M000267936

The Secret of Ebbets Field

©2017 Richard Seidman

Published by Paloma Books

(An imprint of L&R Publishing, LLC)

All rights reserved. No part of this publication may be reproduced or used in any form or by any means, graphic, electronic or mechanical, including photocopying, recording, taping, or information and retrieval systems without written permission of the publisher. In recognition of the paper used to create and market this book, the author will contribute a percentage of the profits to Friends of Trees, the nonprofit tree-planting group he founded in Portland, Oregon, USA. He will also contribute to the Jackie Robinson Foundation that provides scholarships and support services to minority students enrolled in colleges and universities.

Paloma Books
PO Box 3531
Ashland, OR 97520
email: info@palomabooks.com

Cover Design: Rachael R. Resch
Interior Design: L. Redding
Cover Illustration: Ros Webb

"The Dream Keeper," and "Mister Sandman" from THE COLLECTED POEMS OF LANGSTON HUGHES by Langston Hughes, edited by Arnold Rampersad with David Roessel, Associate Editor, copyright © 1994 by the Estate of Langston Hughes. Used by permission of Alfred A. Knopf, an imprint of the Knopf Doubleday Publishing Group, a division of Penguin Random House LLC. All rights reserved.

Cataloging In Publication Data available from the publisher on request.

Printed and bound in the United States of America
First edition 10 9 8 7 6 5 4 3 2 1

To the Heart of Brooklyn

The Secret of Ebbets Field

RICHARD SEIDMAN

PALOMA BOOKS   BOOKS   ASHLAND, OREGON

Bring me all of your dreams,
You dreamers,
Bring me all of your
Heart melodies
That I may wrap them
In a blue cloud-cloth
Away from the too-rough fingers
Of the world.

—Langston Hughes

Chapter 1

THE UNOPENED PACK OF TOPPS BASEBALL cards sat in my palm. *Please let me get a Jackie Robinson.* If I didn't, I was a dead man.

I ripped open the wrapper and popped the stick of gum in my mouth. It tasted like sugar-coated cardboard. Good.

I held my breath as I turned over each card. Bobby Tiefenauer. Dud. Hal Jeffcoat. Bunky Stewart. Willard Schmidt. All duds. Shoot. Only one more to go. *Please.* I flipped over the last card. Jackie Robinson? I stared at the card. Was it really Jackie smiling back at me? Yes!

"Kenny," I yelled to my best friend. "I can't believe it. I got it!"

Now I could pay Domingo back. I owed him two dollars for betting on the Dodgers against the Yankees in the first game of the World Series. A brand new Jackie Robinson card was worth at least that much.

Some of the other boys in the dormitory lifted their heads.

Kenny got off his cot and walked over to look. A cockroach scuttled out of his way.

"Wow, Eli, that's great." Kenny was eleven years old, same as me, chubby with a round, friendly face. "You're lucky. Too bad you have to give it away."

My heart sank. I wouldn't get beat up by Domingo, but I wouldn't get to keep the card of my favorite baseball player, the best player who ever lived. It wasn't fair.

"Yeah, Eli," a snide voice added. "That's great." It was Marty, the dormitory captain. He was a tall sixteen year-old. He had a sneer on his face as usual.

I should have kept my big mouth shut. I hadn't realized he was so close by. Now it was too late.

"Hand it over." Marty reached for the card.

"No way." I held it behind my back.

"Give it, Schwartz."

"Go to hell."

Marty lunged at me and grabbed my arm. I tried to pull away, but he was way bigger and stronger than me. He began prying my fingers off the card.

I jerked my hand back, and the card ripped in half. "You idiot!" My whole body shook.

Marty laughed, tossed his half of the card onto the floor and sauntered away. "You should've let go, Schwartz."

I balled up my half of the card and threw it as hard as I could at Marty's back. It just drifted harmlessly back to the floor. I kicked it and stubbed my toe on the smelly old wood floor. "Ow!"

"What a jerk," Kenny said.

I stared at the wreck of the card at my feet. "Domingo's gonna kill me."

"Maybe he'll give you a few more days to get the money."

Maybe. Domingo was tough but he was fair.

I had made the bet so I could run away from the Bushwick Home for Boys. Thirty dollars would be enough, I figured, to get me settled somewhere. I wouldn't have to worry about Marty and Mr. Reiger. I could have a real home instead of this dump. Someplace without rats and cockroaches. Someplace where the paint wasn't falling off the ceiling and the roof didn't leak. Someplace I belonged.

"I wish I was rich," I told Kenny. "All my problems would be solved if I had money."

He looked at me with raised eyebrows. "I'm not so sure about that."

"Without cash, you're nothing," I said. "Bucks means freedom."

I had to figure out a way to make money. And fast.

Chapter 2

THAT NIGHT I DREAMED I WAS PLAYING for the Dodgers in Ebbets Field.

I stood at home plate staring at the Yankee pitcher.

He fired a fastball.

I swung hard, feeling the solid thunk of the ball on the bat. The ball headed deep toward center field. As I sprinted toward first, I glanced up and saw Mickey Mantle racing back toward the fence, back, back…

The noise of the cheering crowd morphed into a cacophonous metallic banging. I jolted awake.

Mr. Reiger, the owner of the orphanage, was running a baseball bat over the metal posts at the foot of my bed. "Wake up! Get up!" he yelled.

Shoot. It was just like Reiger to ruin my dream. Now, I'd never know if I hit a home run and saved the Dodgers.

I sighed. Instead of being in Ebbets Field, I was lying on a wobbly cot in a dismal orphanage dormitory in a rundown section of Brooklyn. And I owed Domingo Sanchez two dollars.

"In the dining room in ten minutes or no breakfast," Reiger ordered "Understand? Marty, make sure there's no dawdling."

"Sure thing, Mr. Reiger. You heard him. Hurry up!" Marty barked as Reiger left the room.

All the boys in the dorm got out of their bunks and began dressing. I turned to Kenny, who had the cot next to mine. "So it's the bottom of the ninth and I'm up to bat. The Dodgers and all of Brooklyn are depending on me. Hodges is on second — "

Marty overheard me. "Oh right, Schwartz, the Dodgers are really gonna depend on a nutcase like you."

"I wasn't talking to you." I continued to dress, turning my back on him.

"Our hero. Eli Nutcase. Got any more schemes to make a million bucks?"

"Shut up," I snapped.

"Crazy people like you end up bums on the Bowery or in straightjackets at Bellevue. You know that?"

"I said shut up." My hands clenched into fists.

"Ignore him, Eli," Kenny said.

"Come to think of it, a nutcase like you is the perfect hero for a bunch of losers like the Dodgers."

That was too much. I wheeled around. "They aren't losers!"

Marty laughed. "They choke every World Series."

"Until now."

"Yeah, right, Nutcase. They already lost the first two games."

"Last I heard," I told him, "takes four games to win the World Series."

"Oh, the Nutcase knows math."

"It's not worth it," Kenny warned.

I was about to say something else, when Reiger poked his head into the room. "I hope you're not causing more problems, Schwartz. One more fight, just one more, and you're going to rot in the Hole. Do I make myself clear? You will rot there."

"Yes, Mr. Reiger," I muttered. What a jerk he was too. I hated this place!

Reiger left and Marty said to me quietly, "We'll finish this later, Nutcase." He strutted away.

"So what, Reiger sends me to the Hole? Big deal," I said to no one in particular.

"You don't know what you talking about," said James, one of the toughest kids in the orphanage.

"What do you mean?"

"Reiger'll break kids' arms and legs in there. For three days, you just left on the floor with a broken leg, crawling around in your own blood."

"That's just stories." I sure hope it's just stories.

James' buddy, Hank, shook his head. "Remember that big kid, Charlie? Why do you think he walked with a limp?"

"That happens," James added, "kiss your hopes of playing in the Majors goodbye. Dodgers don't want no one with a busted leg."

"And some kids," Hank said, "they can't take solitary. One day in there, they go crazy. Then Reiger sends 'em to the loony bin."

I put on my beat-up old Brooklyn Dodger hat. "Won't happen to me. I got my lucky cap." My voice sounded confident but my stomach churned.

James snorted. "You wind up in the Hole, you'll need a lot more luck than that."

Whether or not I ended up in the Hole, I knew James was right. I needed a lot more luck than I already had.

Chapter 3

I N THE DINING ROOM, TWENTY BOYS crowded around tables eating lukewarm oatmeal for breakfast. A new boy named Luis was sitting with James, Hank, and another kid, Paul. I scanned the room. Domingo was at the far end with a bunch of other big kids. He saw me looking at him and nodded. I nodded back, feeling a little dizzy. Soon I'd have to approach him and beg for more time to repay him.

Mrs. Reiger, a sour-looking woman in her fifties, stood to the side, arms folded, surveying the scene. Then she walked into the kitchen.

Luis was a scrawny little kid, about nine years old. He had shown up at the home two days earlier. He was speaking excitedly when Kenny and I sat down at his table. "The genie, see, he guards the Treasure."

My eyes opened wide. *Treasure*!

"That's why no one can even get close to it," Luis said. "He'll fry 'em to a crisp!"

"Right," Hank smirked.

"What's all this about?" I asked.

"Didn't you hear?" Luis said. "There's a treasure hidden somewhere at Ebbets Field. Worth a million dollars."

A shiver went up my spine and the hairs on the back of my neck stood up.

"It gives you whatever you wish for," said Paul. "You could wish for two million dollars if you wanted to!"

"How do you know about this so-called treasure?" Hank asked.

"My cousin, he told me," said Luis. "Heard about it from Charlie."

"Charlie was probably high on something," James said. "Besides, he's in the slammer."

"No, he got out. My cousin just saw him," Luis said.

"All you have to do is stand with the Treasure on home plate in the full moon and you get your wish," Paul insisted.

I looked from speaker to speaker, mouth open.

"I don't know about the wishes part," Luis said. "I think it's just a regular treasure."

Hank laughed. "You guys don't even know what the treasure is. Gold? Silver? Jewels? Wishes? What?"

"It's magic," Paul said earnestly. "It gives you whatever you wish for. If you want gold, you get gold."

"'It's magic,'" Hank mimicked. "And I'm the Easter Bunny." Hank and James laughed and slapped hands.

"You be readin' too many fairy tale books," James said. "There ain't no magic treasure in Ebbets Field."

"How do you know?" Paul retorted.

James said, "It's bull."

"Then why's everyone talking about it all of a sudden?" Luis asked.

"People talk about all sorts of bull stuff," Hank said. "Santa Claus, for Chris'-sakes."

"You can laugh," Paul said, "but it's there somewhere in Ebbets Field right now, waiting to be found."

"How come no one's found it yet?" Hank snickered.

I had been listening raptly to this conversation. Now I surprised myself by speaking up. "Maybe they weren't looking in the right place." My voice sounded strange in my own ears.

Everyone stared at me.

My face got warm. I looked down at my bowl.

"Or maybe the genie stopped them," Luis explained.

James and Hank guffawed.

I had to admit, it did sound ridiculous.

Paul had a dreamy look on his face. "If I had my wish, I'd wish for a million dollars and a Corvette and a helicopter."

"That's three wishes, idiot," James said.

I turned toward Kenny. "Boy, what I could do with a million dollars!"

"What?"

"I'd get out of this dump. Buy me a big house near Coney Island. You could come live with me. We'd get tickets for the World Series." I smiled at the thought.

Then my shoulders sagged and I snorted at myself. *Who am I kidding?* "Just another bunch of bull."

"You can't be sure about that," Kenny said.

I shrugged and stood up to take my dishes into the kitchen.

Marty blocked my way. "A big house near Coney Island? A padded cell at Bellevue's more like it."

"Get out of my way, jerk," I snarled.

"What'd you call me?"

I tried to step around Marty, but he pushed me. My bowl and cup crashed onto the floor. He snatched the Dodger cap off my head.

"What's this, the Nutcase's 'lucky cap?'"

"Give it back!"

Marty held the cap out of reach as I jumped to grab it. "Higher, boy, higher."

Something burst in my brain. *I'll kill him.* I reared back and tackled Marty around the waist.

He stumbled against the wall, knocking down a photo of an old man scowling out over the dining room. The photo fell with a crash of breaking glass.

Marty and I grappled on the floor. His strong hands pinned my shoulders down, but I was slippery and wriggled out of his grasp.

The other kids cheered and yelled.

I felt the portrait tear under my thrashing feet. Marty and I scrambled up and rushed at each other again.

Mr. and Mrs. Reiger dashed into the room before either of us could land any blows. "Stop!" Reiger ordered.

Marty's foot slipped on a piece of the torn photo. He tumbled backwards, and his head hit the wood floor with a thud.

I picked up my hat from where it had fallen on the floor.

Reiger grabbed me by the collar.

Rage still pulsed through my body like an electric

current. "Let me go!" I kicked Reiger in the shin. "He stole my hat."

Reiger punched me hard on the jaw. I staggered sideways. I saw stars and almost conked out. *Don't cry. Don't cry.*

Mrs. Reiger gasped when she noticed the ruined portrait. She rushed to pick up the torn pieces, and cradled them in her arms. "Papa!"

"Get up, Marty," Reiger commanded.

Marty lay motionless. Reiger let go of me. He rushed to the fallen boy, feeling for a pulse. "Call for an ambulance."

One of the older boys headed to the office to make the phone call.

The other children gathered round Marty in shocked silence.

"That's it, Schwartz," Reiger snarled. "I warned you."

"He started it."

"We'll see how you like three days in the Hole."

"Three days? It's not fair." An icy tentacle of terror wove around my chest, making it hard for me to breathe. I found myself panting. No one had ever spent three days down there.

"I'm the one who decides what's fair around here. Give me that hat."

Before I could react, Reiger snatched it off my head and stuffed it in his pocket. He pulled out a set of keys, grabbed me by the shirt collar, and started dragging me out of the room. I stumbled along with him in a daze.

As I walked by Marty he opened one eye a crack and smirked at me. The creep!

Down in the basement, Reiger unlocked a door and

pushed me into the Hole. "I'll take care of you when I get back." He slammed the door and locked it.

I punched the metal door. Ow! I sunk onto the damp concrete floor, holding my hand. The Hole smelled of pee, mildew, and fear.

I huddled in the dark, trying not to cry.

Chapter 4

THE HOLE WAS ALMOST PITCH BLACK. I waved my fingers in front of my eyes and could barely make them out in the gloom. I couldn't hear anything either, except my heart pounding and the blood pulsing in my ears.

"Hey," I yelled. My voice seemed to get swallowed by the dark. "Hey," I yelled louder. But the darkness absorbed all sound. The darkness was absorbing *me*. "Hey! Hey! Hey!" I screamed as loud as I could. Now I understood how kids had gone crazy in here. And it was just a matter of time until Reiger came back. "Don't panic. Don't panic," I kept saying to myself. "Keep breathing. You'll think of something."

Eventually, I dozed off. Once again I dreamed I was at bat for the Dodgers.

I stared at the pitcher, Bob Turley. He half-grinned, half-snarled back at me. He reared back and threw. I saw right away it was off target and I let it go past. The ball thudded into the catcher's mitt.

Even though I was on the field, in the dream I could hear the radio announcer. *"Low and outside,"* he said. *"Ball one. He's a cool customer, this kid. They say the only thing that frightens him is heights. He certainly hasn't been daunted by major league pitching."*

On the next pitch, I swung a bit early and hit a foul ball into the stands behind third base.

"Foul," the announcer said. *"The count is 1 and 1. And here comes Coach Alston for a word with Schwartz."*

Dense fog suddenly descended over the field. The sounds of the crowd became weirdly muffled and distorted. I stepped out of the batter's box and squinted through the swirling mist in the direction of the dugout.

The manager trotted toward me. When he got close enough for me to see, I stared at him. "You're not Coach."

"I'm your father."

"I don't know my father." I felt that familiar sensation whenever I thought of the father I couldn't remember. It was like a cave in the pit of my stomach. "He's dead, I think."

"Go to Ebbets Field and find the Treasure."

"I'm already in Ebbets Field," I said.

He gestured around the ballpark. The fog floated right through his arm. "Go to Ebbets Field and find the Treasure," he repeated.

The umpire yelled, "Play ball!"

A huge gust of wind blew both the fog and the manager away, revealing the players in the field, the spectators in the stands, and the pitcher on the mound rubbing the ball.

I shook my head to clear it, and stepped back into the batter's box. "Weird," I thought.

Turley looked at the catcher for the signal and nodded.

"Schwartz has been key to the Dodgers' success all year," the announcer exclaimed. *"Can he save Brooklyn now?"*

Turley reared back and threw.

I woke up, my heart beating a mile a minute. Something was scratching on the door of the Hole. I jumped to my feet. Was it Reiger coming back to "take care" of me?

"Eli? You all right?"

Whew. It was only Kenny.

I sighed. "Yeah, I'm okay." I rubbed my jaw where Reiger had socked me. "What're you doing down here? You'll get in trouble if Reiger catches you."

"He left three minutes ago."

"I gotta get out of here and go to Ebbets Field."

"What!"

"I had another dream," I told him. My father came and told me to go to Ebbets Field and find the Treasure."

"How will you even get in?"

"This kid on the street last year. He told me a way to sneak in."

"Wow," Kenny said.

Suddenly, the plan became clear to me. I stopped pacing. "You know the pack under my bed?"

"Yeah?"

"I got me a skeleton key in there. Leroy gave it to me. Said it used to belong to Charlie when he lived here. Don't know if it would work on the door to the Hole, but it's worth a try if you're willing to risk it."

"Charlie probably used it for some of his robberies," Kenny said. "Okay. Wait here."

"Like where would I go?"

We both laughed.

I paced in a small circle. Finally, the key jiggled in the lock. The door slowly opened. I crouched down, ready to make a run for it if it was Reiger. But Kenny's face squinted into the gloom, and I breathed out.

"It worked!" he said, staring at the key.

"Thank you, Charlie, wherever you are," I said. "And thank you, Kenny. You're a brave man."

He blushed.

We tiptoed up the stairs from the basement and peeked out the door. All the kids were in the workroom, sewing. The orphanage doubled as a sweatshop. Kenny and I crept up the stairway to the deserted dormitory room. My heart beat hard.

I ran to my cot and pulled out the cardboard box underneath it that held my stuff. Kenny kept guard by the door. I fished out a beat-up old Boy Scout knapsack I'd found on the street. I stuffed into the pack the two sets of worn hand-me-down clothes the Reigers had provided, and a couple of shirts I had traded other kids for. My mind felt strangely blank.

I packed a small flashlight in the shape of a baseball bat. I reached behind a loose board in the wall and removed a glass jar, my secret bank. I emptied pennies, nickels, and dimes onto the cot. "Forty-two cents." I scooped up the change and put it in my pocket. "I wanted to have more money before I ran away, but I guess this will have to do. After I get into Ebbets Field, who knows? Maybe I can get a job working for the Dodgers."

"If you get caught, Reiger'll really kill you."

"I better not get caught, then. Hey, tell Domingo I promise to pay him back someday, okay? When I find the

Treasure, I'll share the money with you, Kenny. And you can come live with me."

"Thanks, Eli."

I swung the pack onto my shoulders. I hesitated. "You don't think I'm a nutcase, do you?"

He stared at me. "A nutcase? Are you crazy?"

We laughed, covering our mouths with our hands so no one would hear us.

"Thanks for everything, Kenny," I said when we finally stopped laughing. There was an awkward pause. "Well, goodbye."

"What are you talking about, 'goodbye'?" He pulled out a bulging pillowcase from under his cot. "No way I'm gonna let you have all that fun without me. Already packed. I knew you were planning something. Plus it's the World Series, man. The Dodgers need us."

I grinned at him. "All right!"

We peered around a corner and snuck down the hall. "First, I got to get my hat back." My voice shook.

We made our way to Reiger's office, and slipped in. Once again, Kenny stood guard, peeking out the not-fully-shut door.

I saw my cap on Reiger's desk, and put it on. It felt good to have my luck back. I noticed a folder on the desk with my name on it.

"Come on!" Kenny urged.

"Wait a second. It's my official file. The one Reiger's always reporting me in."

"We don't have time."

I knew he was right, but I couldn't help myself. My curiosity was too great. I opened the folder. "Listen to this.

'June 21, 1944. Infant brought to home by courier with letter and two photos (enclosed). Parents presumed dead in Europe. Aunt's whereabouts unknown.'" I looked up at Kenny. "I knew in my gut my parents were dead, but I didn't know I had an aunt."

Kenny was getting more and more nervous. His right foot jiggled like crazy. "Hurry up."

I pulled out a couple of photos. "There's pictures."

"He's coming!" Kenny hissed.

Chapter 5

"IN HERE," I WHISPERED. I grabbed the photos, and we ducked into a closet seconds before Reiger entered. Through a crack in the door, I watched him reach into a desk drawer, pull out a flask and take a long drink. He put my folder into a file cabinet and locked the drawer. He didn't seem to notice that my hat was missing. A vein in my skull pulsed hard.

Reiger dialed the phone. "It's me...Put a grand on Starburst...Yeah, I know he's 40 to 1. Just say I got me an inside tip....Okay, good. Look, I got to deal with one of my brats." He laughed and took another pull on the flask and placed it back in the desk drawer. "Starburst. Yeah."

Reiger hung up the phone. He chuckled to himself as he headed out the door. His footsteps echoed down the hall. I breathed out. I hadn't even realized I'd been holding my breath.

Kenny and I rushed to a window. We couldn't risk going out into the hall. We had to move fast. In a minute, Reiger would discover I was missing. I pried the window open and we slipped out, dropping to the ground. Keeping low, like the guys in WW II movies, we dashed toward the bushes separating the orphanage from the house next door.

We tore through the bushes, through the backyard, down the alley behind it, past an apartment house, and out to the busy street on the next block.

By the time we made it to Flatbush Avenue I was drenched in sweat. We darted past shoppers and shopkeepers; past mothers pushing baby carriages; past guys hanging out on stoops, smoking cigarettes and playing cards.

We ran through a mixture of sounds; cars and trucks honked; people laughed, swore, and argued in English, Spanish, Italian, and Yiddish; a mix of rhythm and blues, jazz, and Puerto Rican music filled the streets from radios and jukeboxes.

Sometimes the sidewalk was too crowded and we had to step out into the road. We dodged the trucks and trolleys that honked and clanged their way down the Brooklyn street.

Finally, we slowed to a walk. We had done it. We had escaped. I gave a little whoop.

"Reiger's playing the horses," Kenny said, panting.

"Nothing illegal about that."

"I guess," he said. "Something about it sounded fishy, though."

"Everything about that guy seems fishy to me."

"Yeah," Kenny agreed. "And his wife is a crab."

We laughed as we walked past fruit stands, butcher

shops, bagel bakeries, and all sorts of people working and shopping. We cut across a vacant lot where a crude baseball diamond was scratched into the dirt and torn pieces of cardboard served as bases. We pretended Kenny was the pitcher and I was the batter. As we played, we sang the Count Basie song:

Did you see Jackie Robinson hit that ball?
Well he hit it, yeah, and that ain't all.
He stole home.
Yes, yes, Jackie's real gone.

Satchel Paige is mellow
And so is Campanella,
Newcombe and Doby too.
But it's a natural fact
When Jackie comes to bat,
The other team is through.

Did you see Jackie Robinson hit that ball?
Well he hit it, yeah, and that ain't all.
He's going home.
Yes, yes, Jackie's real gone.
Yes, yes, Jackie's real gone.

I ran around the bases singing, sliding into home plate under Kenny's imaginary tag just as the song ended.

"You're out!" Kenny called.

"No way. You missed me."

"No I didn't," Kenny laughed. "You were out by a mile."

"Safe," I yelled, smiling.

We got up, dusted ourselves off and kept walking. Next to the vacant lot was a neighborhood of warehouses. Big trucks pulled in and out of cargo bays. We asked a truck driver how to get to Ebbets Field.

"Shortest way is to take that trestle over there," he said, pointing out a railroad bridge rising in the distance. "Enjoy the game, boys. Wish I was going, too."

My stomach clenched as we neared the trestle. It ran for maybe a half mile, spanning an industrial area of factories and smokestacks and more trucks. Next to the train tracks was an old wooden plank walkway about two feet across. Between each plank was a six-inch gap.

"Cool," Kenny exclaimed, as he strode out onto the boards.

I followed him slowly, testing each board to be sure it could hold my weight. Some of them looked rotten. I gripped the wooden handrail so tightly my knuckles turned white. After venturing out about twenty feet, I glanced down through the gap between two planks. Far below, a truck backed up. My head swam and my knees almost buckled.

Kenny was already way ahead of me.

"Wait up," I called.

He trotted back to me, as if dangling high above the ground on flimsy boards was something he did every day. "What's up?"

"Let's go down and around, okay? I, uh, would just rather go around. We got enough time."

"You afraid of heights?"

I shook my head no.

Kenny looked at me for a second, then smiled. "Okay. Come on."

We turned around and walked off the trestle. My stomach unclenched. We scrambled down a gravelly embankment toward the street.

"I have an aunt," I said, after we had wound our way through the maze of buildings and vehicles beneath the trestle, and walked through a more residential neighborhood. "Maybe she's rich!

I suddenly stopped walking. "And Reiger never told me." My hands balled into fists and I kicked hard at a soda can on the sidewalk. It rattled into the street.

"The orphanage gets money from the State of New York for each kid," Kenny said. "That big jerk probably never even looked for her."

A spark of hope kindled within my chest. "I'm gonna find her."

"How?"

I had no idea.

Just then, we rounded a corner. "Look!" I cried.

Chapter 6

ABOUT TEN BLOCKS AWAY, THE BRICK front of Ebbets Field, like a magnificent church, soared over the nearby buildings. They seemed drab and plain compared to its magical grandeur. Red, white, and blue bunting was draped near the top.

We ran toward the park. My head felt light. It was like running in a dream. As we neared the entrance, the crowds got thicker and slowed us to a walk. Men, women, and children poured out of trolley cars and emerged from subway stations. Everyone seemed as eager and excited as us.

Then, there it was, right in front of us. Kenny and I stopped and gaped. People pushed past us on both sides. This close, the walls looked enormous. It was like something from a storybook.

"Get a move on, will ya?" someone muttered behind us.

We snapped out of our trance and resumed walking, past people hawking hats, pennants, shirts, programs. The noise and the colors made me dizzy. I had been out on the streets before, but never this far away from the orphanage, and never among this many people. Brooklyn, I realized, was a really big place.

I led Kenny past the main entrance and headed down McKeever Place. The crowds thinned out on this side of the building.

"Look, when we get in, let's go high up in the second tier. Get a bird's eye view of the field from there," Kenny suggested.

"Nah," I said, "let's stay closer to the field, okay?"

"Oh, I forgot. You're scared of heights."

"I'm not scared." I scanned the imposing brick walls. "I think the kid said somewhere around here, on the third base side."

"What're we looking for?"

"A crack in the wall. Too small for a grown-up, but big enough for a child. He didn't really say where, exactly."

"Oh great," Kenny said in a high-pitched voice. I knew that meant he was getting nervous.

A cop came strolling down the street toward us, twirling his baton.

We walked past him, trying not to look too guilty.

He stared at us as he passed by.

A little further down the block I stopped and nodded my head toward the building. An old wooden door was set into the brick wall. Between the door jam and the bricks was a gap about eight inches wide, covered with metal mesh. I waited until no one was nearby, looked up and down the sidewalk, and grabbed the mesh. To my surprise, it was loose on one end and I could bend it to the side.

We scanned the sidewalk one more time, then I took off my pack, handed it to Kenny, and squeezed through the narrow gap.

Kenny handed my pack to me and gave me his pillowcase. Then, he tried to squeeze in. He grunted and pushed his way into the gap.

"Draw in your breath," I whispered.

"I can't. I'm stuck!" His breathing was becoming more and more frantic. His voice was higher than ever. He was starting to panic.

"You can do it, Kenny. You're almost through." I grabbed his arm and pulled him. I heard the sound of his coat ripping, and he broke free. We tumbled onto the ground together.

"Oh man," Kenny exclaimed, still lying on the ground. "Mrs. Reiger's gonna be ticked off when she sees I tore my coat."

For some reason, that set us off. We looked at each other and laughed until we cried. Did Kenny really think we'd be going back to the orphanage? No way was I going there again.

When we recovered, we stood up and gazed around. We were in a dimly-lit cavernous netherworld, a kind of no-man's land under the stands. Corridors branched out from the open area, leading further into the gloom.

As we stood there, trying to figure out which way to go, we heard footsteps running toward us. A burly man was heading our way. He must have been some kind of under-the-stands watchman.

"Hey, you kids! Hold it right there!"

Chapter 7

KENNY AND I TOOK OFF RUNNING. We sprinted down the main corridor. The crowd murmured in the stands above us and the guard panted behind us.

At a crossroads, Kenny and I split up. Kenny continued running straight. I turned to the right, heading down a narrow, twisting corridor. I spotted some big cardboard boxes lined up against a wall and crouched down behind them, breathing hard. The footsteps of Kenny and the watchman echoed in the dimness of the main chamber.

Kenny made a kind of squeal, and I knew he had been caught.

The man grunted with satisfaction. "Got you, you little punk."

Their footsteps headed back in my direction.

I had to do something to help Kenny. He and the man walked right past the corridor where I was hiding. I jumped out from behind the boxes. "Hey Copper!" I yelled. "Yeah, you, you big oaf."

The man wheeled around. He hesitated a moment. "Stay here," he ordered Kenny. Then he took off after me.

"Run, Kenny. Go!" I yelled.

"Hey!" the watchman bellowed as Kenny raced away. I guessed, correctly, that the guard now wanted to catch me more than he did Kenny. But I was faster than him. I raced through the tunnel-like passageway beneath the stands, with him wheezing further and further behind me. His footsteps slowed down and finally stopped completely. He swore, and the footsteps slogged their way back toward the main corridor.

Where had Kenny gone? If I didn't spot him in the ballpark somewhere during the game, I'd look for him on the streets afterwards. "Afterwards." I hadn't really thought what I would do after the game. Where I'd live. Where I'd go. I guess it depended on how long it would take me to find the Treasure. Oh well, right now, there was a World Series game to watch.

Which way should I go to get up to the stands? It was like a maze down there. I came to a crossroads and hesitated. Then I felt like someone was pushing me gently on my back to steer me to the left. I actually looked behind me, but no one was there. Weird.

I took a few steps down the corridor when I heard angry voices coming from somewhere close by. Who would be all the way down here? A thin stream of light escaped through a crack in an old wooden wall. The voices were coming from in there. I peeked through the crack into a dingy room lit by a single bare light bulb.

A tough-looking but pretty young woman smoking a cigarette was arguing with a large, mean-faced man. "I don't like it," she said.

"It'll serve the nigger right."

"Our job is to make sure the Yankees win. Not to injure Jackie Robinson."

The man laughed. "Boss don't care how we arrange it as long as his clients win their bets. And the Dodgers might play a little nervous if Jackie Robinson had an 'accident' right at Ebbets Field."

"It's dumb. Dangerous and dumb. Like you, Parton."

"You little —"

He approached her menacingly. The woman didn't flinch.

A second man, in his late teens, entered the room from a back door and paced into my view. He had slicked-back hair and wild eyes. He walked with a limp.

I gasped. It was Charlie! The teenager who used to live at the orphanage, who'd been in the slammer and said there was a treasure.

"About time," the big guy muttered.

"What are you, Parton, my mother?" Charlie turned to the woman. "Hi Joan."

"Hi Baby," Joan said, smiling at him. She walked up to Charlie and kissed him hard on the mouth.

The man called Parton spit on the ground. "We got a job to do."

"I'm out," Charlie said.

"What're you talkin' about, Charlie?" Joan asked.

"Do it without me," Charlie said.

"Punkin' out on us?" Parton taunted.

"I ain't punkin' out on nobody."

"Sure seems like it."

"So you break Jackie's leg. Boss pays you three hundred bucks. Chump change," Charlie said.

"Baby —" Joan began.

"The hell with that. I'm gonna find me the Treasure. Make a million."

In my hiding place, I gasped again when I heard the word "treasure." Once again, the hairs rose on the back of my neck. I put my hand over my mouth, praying they hadn't heard me. I pressed my eye even closer to the hole.

Parton laughed. "And with that much bread, you could get your kicks without having to come crawling to the boss, doin' his dirty work?" He spit on the ground. "Boss won't care for that plan. Unless he gets most of the dough. You'll still wind up with only a few hundred bucks. If you're lucky."

Charlie rubbed his lame leg. "The hell with the boss."

"This 'treasure'?" Parton said with a smirk, "Ain't so easy to find something that don't even exist."

"It exists all right," Charlie replied grimly.

"What makes you so sure?"

"Problem with you, Parton, is you got no imagination."

Parton snorted. "Still ain't answered my question."

"Nobody's forcing you to believe anything," Charlie said.

"What if the whole thing is a bunch of bull?" Parton said. "That ever occur to you?"

Joan asked, "So what is this treasure, Charlie? Gold? Diamonds? Cash?" She put her arm around Charlie. "They all sound good to me."

Parton laughed. "It's a buggin' fairy story. What happened to you in the slammer, Charlie? Gone soft in the head? Still believin' that crap at your age."

Charlie suddenly pushed Joan away. He grabbed Parton by his coat and rammed him hard against the wall right next to where I was peeking. I flinched, but kept looking. Just inches from my eye, a switchblade knife gleamed at Parton's throat. I held my breath.

Charlie spoke softly and calmly, but there was murder in his eyes. "Never say that again, Parton."

"Okay, okay. Jeez," Parton said.

Just then, Charlie pivoted quickly as someone entered the room.

"Boss!" the woman cried.

Charlie folded his knife.

The boss walked into my line of sight. He was a short, well-dressed man. In a brown suit and derby hat, he looked out of place in the dingy, dirty room. He seemed dangerous despite his fancy clothing. He looked from Charlie to Parton. "Problem, gentlemen?"

"No problem," Charlie said.

Parton smirked. "Except Charlie punkin' out."

"I ain't punkin' out."

The boss stared at Charlie. "I should hope not. It would be so sad if *you* met with an accident."

Charlie and the boss glared at one another.

Joan broke the silence. "Look, what's the plan?"

The boss explained. "If the Dodgers lose today, we sit tight. There's no way they're going to win four straight. We'll get our money without having to do anything. But if they win today, we take action."

"What kind of action?" Joan asked.

"You'll figure it out," said the boss. "Right, Parton?"

"Right," the big man said.

The boss looked at Charlie. "You in or not, Charlie? Cause if you're out, you're really out."

Charlie stared at the ground. "Yeah, I'm in."

The boss smiled. "Excellent." He turned to leave the room, not by the door he had used to enter but by another door, which I hadn't noticed until then. This door was only a few feet from where I was spying on them in the hallway!

I had to get away before he opened it and discovered me eavesdropping. I spun around and knocked over a wooden crate. It fell with a crash. I hurtled blindly down the hall.

Parton yelled from inside the room. "What the hell was that?"

Chapter 8

FOOTSTEPS RUSHED TOWARD THE DOOR.

I sprinted down the narrow, winding, dark corridor.

"That way!" the boss called, somewhere behind me.

The corridor had many twists and turns. *Please let me stay out of their sight,* I prayed. Their footsteps got louder. I came to a flight of stairs and raced up. My legs ached and my lungs burned. After I climbed a flight and a half, footsteps clanged on the metal steps below me.

As I rounded a landing, the sound of the crowd outside got louder. Daylight streamed from behind a wooden door at the top of one more flight of stairs. I dashed up and burst through the door. It crashed open against the wall.

I blinked rapidly in the sudden sunlight. I was in the stands behind third base. Gasping for air, I raced to an empty seat and plopped into it.

Parton and Joan erupted out of the door and gaped around them, blinking in the sun. Charlie came limping after them. They split up. Parton headed right toward me.

I sunk down low in my seat, trying to be invisible.

Parton ran past me. I breathed out in relief. As he ran by, the big thug bumped hard into a young woman. The collision knocked a note pad and a bunch of papers out of her arms onto the ground. Parton rushed on without an apology.

"Jerk!" the woman yelled after him.

I helped her gather the papers. I noticed she was wearing a badge that said, "Press." "Are you a reporter?"

"Yeah."

"I didn't know there were lady sportswriters."

"I'm not a sportswriter. I'm on the family beat." The way she said it I could tell she was not happy with the assignment. "Doin' a story on fashions of the World Series."

I didn't know what to say, so all I said was, "Oh."

"What I really want to write is crime stories, exposés." She stared me in the eyes. She was very pretty. She sighed. "But the boss says it's not a woman's job. So I'm stuck writing about dresses and hats."

All the papers gathered, we stood up. If she wanted to write crime stories, maybe she could help with Jackie. "I heard these bad guys," I began. "They're planning to hurt—"

But the woman wasn't listening. "Look, I'm on a deadline. Got to run. Thanks for helping me. You're a doll."

"But—"

She rushed off before I could say more. I stared after her. Then, I looked around for Parton, Charlie, and Joan. I didn't see them anywhere.

I took a deep breath and looked at the field. I had made

it! I was in Ebbets Field! I wasn't dreaming. I was actually here. And it was the World Series! The game was about to start. And no one was around to boss me.

For the first time, I took in what was happening all around me. Fans were finding their seats while vendors called out:

"Hot dogs heah."

"Peanuts. Peanuts."

"Cold beer. Getya cold beer."

From their place near the Dodger dugout, the Dodger Sym-Phony Band squawked and thumped away. They were a ragtag group that included trombone, trumpet, cymbals, and bass drum. They began a comic, off-key version of "Take Me Out to the Ball Game."

On the field, players warmed up. A few stood near the foot of the stands, signing programs thrust out over the railing.

"Jackie!" I gasped when I spotted Jackie Robinson signing autographs on the edge of the field. I'd have to look around for Kenny later. First, I needed to warn Jackie. I squeezed my way through the crowded stands toward the knot of kids holding out their programs, all of them clamoring for Jackie's attention.

The cluster of autograph seekers was so thick I couldn't even get close to the field. "Jackie! Jackie!" I yelled. "I got to talk to you." My small voice was lost in the noise of the crowd and the blare of the Sym-Phony. I tried in vain to push my way closer. "Jackie, they're gonna get you. Please!"

Just then someone on the field told Jackie something, probably that the game was about to begin. He abruptly stopped signing autographs and walked into the dugout. Ushers came forward to disperse the children. Since I didn't have a ticket, I quickly retreated.

The umpires trotted onto the field, and the Dodger Symphony played a few bars of "Three Blind Mice." The crowd roared with laughter.

I headed toward the cheap seats in the bleachers. The ushers would be less likely to bother me there.

The stadium announcer boomed, "Please rise as Mrs. Gladys Gooding plays our national anthem."

Everyone stood up. The men took off their hats. As the organ music swelled out over the stands, many people sang along.

A policeman nearby leaned against a post and flirted with a woman who had her back to me. I hesitated a moment, then approached him. I was scared of cops in general, and what if he asked to see my ticket? But I had to tell someone about the danger to Jackie.

I was about to tap the cop on the shoulder when the woman he was talking with turned slightly. It was Joan! I saw her slip a ten-dollar bill into the cop's pocket.

"I'll keep my eye out. Don't worry, Joanie," he reassured her with a wink.

"You're a champ, Bill," Joanie purred.

I backed away quickly. Shoot. Now they got the cops looking for me, too. Maybe the thugs had seen me after all.

The crowd sang, "O'er the land of the free and the home of the brave." Then everyone cheered and sat down.

The stadium announcer pronounced, "And now, to throw out the first ball of the game, the President of the Brooklyn Dodgers, Walter O'Malley!"

The crowd applauded politely. A few people booed. I remembered hearing that O'Malley didn't like black people. He was a large jowly man with slick hair parted in the middle. He stood up in his box seat near the Dodger dugout. He waved to the crowd, beaming. Then he threw the ball a few feet to Dodger catcher, Roy Campanella. Campanella caught the ball and trotted over to shake O'Malley's hand. They paused, hands clasped, for a photograph. The photo done, O'Malley's smile instantly disappeared and a cold look took its place. He wiped his hand on his suit pants.

Campanella headed onto the field, and the game began. I continued walking toward the bleachers to find a safe spot to watch the game. I found an empty seat toward the back of the bleachers away from ushers and cops. I took my pack off and held it in my lap. I settled in to watch the game, scan the crowd, look for Kenny, and wait for a chance to warn Jackie.

Billie Martin struck out. The Sym-Phony played "The Worms Crawl in and the Worms Crawl Out," and everyone laughed. It was amazing to me that I was actually watching the game in person, not just listening to it on a radio and imagining it.

A man behind me yelled, "Serves ya right, ya little runt." Martin headed back to the Yankee dugout. Just as he sat down on the dugout bench, the Sym-Phony let out a loud "blatt" on trombone and drum. The crowd laughed.

The next Yankee batter, Gil McDougald hit a fly ball to center field that Duke Snider caught with no problem.

Yogi Berra approached the plate.

A burst of applause and cheers erupted in the nearby seats. A heavyset, middle-aged woman had unfurled a banner that read, "Hilda is here." *She must be Hilda Chester.* I had heard about this legendary Dodger fan. She rang two loud cowbells, one in each hand, and yelled, "Hey Yogi, your pants are falling down!"

Another fan, dressed like a cartoon bum, gave a loud raspberry as Berra flied out to right. The Dodgers trotted off the field.

By the seventh inning, the Dodgers were ahead 6 to 3. Jackie Robinson was on-deck as Pee Wee Reese batted. This was my chance.

Keeping an eye out for the police, and Parton, Joan, and Charlie, I made my way through the stands. I headed to the bottom row, near where Jackie knelt, waiting for his turn at bat. When I was as close as I could get, just in front of Walter O'Malley's box seat, I yelled, "Jackie!" My thin, piping voice was swallowed up in the uproar of the stadium. I called more desperately. "Jackie. You got to listen to me! You're in trouble."

Walter O'Malley looked sharply at me.

Jackie threw his warm-up bats to the side and stood up to approach home plate. He glanced in my direction, and for a wild instant I thought he was going to come over and hear what I had to say. But he looked away and walked toward the plate.

Frustrated, I kicked a cup near my feet. I thought it was empty, but there was still some soda in it. The cup flew in the air, spraying Coca Cola all over Walter O'Malley.

You idiot!" he bellowed.

I fled up the stairs.

Behind me, O'Malley yelled to someone, "Catch that kid!"

Chapter 9

LOOKED OVER MY SHOULDER. An usher had jumped up to chase me, but he collided with a Coke vendor. The vendor's tray full of soda cups went flying in the air and several cups fell directly onto O'Malley, drenching him in Coca Cola. Nearby spectators laughed while O'Malley sputtered with fury.

I escaped into the crowd and squeezed back into a seat in the bleachers. That was close. My breathing returned to normal. I'd almost been caught by the Dodgers president! Wait, I groaned, I could have told O'Malley about the danger Jackie was facing. Now it was too late. I didn't dare show my face to him once again.

By the ninth inning, the Dodgers were leading 8 to 3. When Johnny Podres got the last Yankee out, the stadium erupted in a raucous celebration of victory. A tall man next to me pounded my back and yelled, "That's one! That's one! We only need three more!"

Happy spectators streamed out of the park as Gladys Gooding played the "Follow the Dodgers" theme song on the organ. I watched fathers and sons and whole families leave the stands together, some hand in hand. One mother playfully tousled the hair of a boy about my age. A father hugged his son. I sighed. I couldn't even imagine what that would feel like. But if I found the Treasure, it wouldn't matter. I wouldn't need a mother or father or orphanage. I could live wherever I wanted and do whatever I wanted.

When I bent down to pick up a discarded program, I saw a nickel lying beside it. That gave me an idea. As the park emptied out, I scavenged under the seats for change that had fallen out of peoples' pockets. After I had gathered $2.95, I spotted a vendor who was still selling to the stragglers leaving the ballpark. With my newfound coins, I bought peanuts and Cracker Jacks.

I fed a few of the peanuts to a flock of pigeons that had descended after most of the people had left. One pigeon had a blue head. It looked to me like the bird was wearing a Dodgers cap. The pigeon cocked his head and stared at me. I cocked my head at the same angle and laughed.

I looked around the park for Kenny, in case he was lingering too. No sign of him, and thankfully, none of Charlie and his gang either.

I managed to find the same door I had burst out of earlier that afternoon. Maybe Kenny was waiting for me back under the stands. On this side of the door it was marked, "NO ADMITTANCE." I checked to see that no one was looking, then ducked through the door into the gloom of the under-the-stands netherworld. *Please let me stay out of sight of the thugs.*

The dim corridors appeared to be deserted. I stood still and listened. No voices or footsteps. As quietly as I could, I crept down the halls, trying to find my way to the opening where Kenny and I had snuck in. After a few wrong turns and backtrackings, I came to the central hall. No sign of any watchmen.

There was the place where we had entered. "Shoot," I swore under my breath when I got there. The wire I had so easily pushed aside to get in had now been welded to a metal post. It wouldn't budge. The secret entrance had been sealed. Now I was afraid to leave the park because I might never be able to get back in.

Was Kenny waiting for me out on the streets? Had he gotten caught and was he back at the orphanage? There was nothing I could do to track him down now. At least not until I figured out how to warn Jackie. "Good luck, Kenny," I whispered. "I'll find you as soon as I can."

I was really on my own now. For the first time in my life, I wasn't surrounded by people. I was in Ebbets Field and I was free. It was scary and dangerous and kind of lonely, but it was better than worrying about Reiger and Marty all the time.

I turned around and tiptoed back across the main hallway and into one of the narrow, snaking corridors. Some big pieces of plywood leaning at an angle against the wall provided a good hiding place. With a few broken-down cardboard boxes, I covered the cold concrete.

Hidden behind the plywood, I leaned back against the wall. How could I contact Jackie in the morning? *Please let me think of something before it's too late.*

After I warned Jackie, then I would find Kenny and turn my attention to tracking down the treasure. I had to locate it before Charlie did. Everything depended on that.

I took out the program I'd found, ate my peanuts and

Cracker Jacks, and read the program in the murky light. When I finished, I curled up on the cardboard and rested my head on the pillow of my knapsack. I was worn out from all the adventures of the day.

A few hours later, I woke with a start. Disoriented, I rubbed my eyes. It was dark now that daylight didn't filter in from distant windows.

Yawning and shivering, I reached into my pack for my jacket. As I pulled the coat out of the pack, the photographs and note I had taken from my folder on Reiger's desk fell out. I fished out my little baseball bat flashlight and examined the photos. One showed a man, a woman, and a baby. My jaw fell open. I knew right away they were my father, mother, and me.

The other photo showed two women. One was my mother. The other woman looked similar to my mom but younger. I read the inscription on the back: "Sylvia and Esther, Strasbourg, France 1939."

I placed the photos down and held a weathered piece of paper closer to my flashlight. I read the letter:

May 18, 1944. Dear Esther. We've been hiding in the back of a barn. It's been okay so far. The baby is well, and I'm feeling stronger. But we heard a rumor that someone tipped off the Nazis about our location. They'll find us before long. Joachim knows a Gentile man, a courier, who says he can smuggle Eli to you in America (for a hefty price, of course). If you receive this letter and these photos, it will mean he has been successful, and little Eli will be safe with you, thank God. After the war, God-willing, we will meet you in Brooklyn. I have to go now. I will always love you. Your sister, Sylvia.

I studied the photos some more. My mother. My father. My aunt. Me as an infant. Incredible. I turned off the flashlight and leaned back against the wall. I grabbed a handful of peanuts, cracked them open, and ate them. Seeing the images of my parents opened an ache in my chest.

The letter and photos must have been pinned to my shirt or in my crib or something when I first showed up at the orphanage. The courier, I guessed, couldn't find my aunt, or didn't even try and just left me off somewhere, and I wound up at the orphanage. I was less than a year old then, and now I couldn't really remember my parents or anything about life in France. All I had was the photos and note and an empty, aching feeling.

A jolt went through my body as my history clicked into place. I was born in France. And my parents were probably killed by Nazis. And they had loved me and tried to save me. They hadn't just thrown me away and forgotten about me. They loved me! For at least a little bit of my life, I had been loved. Somehow, I knew in my bones that both of my parents were dead. But maybe, somewhere out there, I had an aunt who still loved me.

Did Reiger even try to locate my aunt? Probably not. My hands balled into fists at the thought, and I stifled a shout of rage.

Footsteps ringing in the distance shook me from these thoughts. Immediately, my heart began racing. The beam of a flashlight pierced the gloom. For a crazy moment, I imagined that a Nazi Gestapo officer was coming to get me. No, it must be the night watchman making his rounds.

Whoever it was, he was heading down the corridor straight toward my hiding spot!

Chapter 10

I HUDDLED BACK AS FAR AS POSSIBLE behind the plywood boards. The footsteps came closer. They stopped just on the other side of my shelter. I held my breath. I wished my heart wasn't thumping so loudly.

The man sniffed the air. Could he smell the peanuts? Or was it just his instincts telling him something was unusual down here? He breathed heavily, only a few feet away from me. The flashlight beam probed up and down the corridor. Finally, the man walked on. Thank God he didn't think to look behind the plywood.

I let out my breath and peeked out. A fat old guy with a lot of keys dangling from his belt was shuffling away down the hall.

An hour later, I was sound asleep again and dreaming.

I'm playing catch with my father and mother and aunt. My mother wears a purple dress and my aunt wears a white one. My father throws a high pop-up. I almost lose sight of the ball in the sun, but I make the catch. My mother and aunt applaud.

Off to the side, I catch a glimpse of someone else clapping his hands. He's an elderly black man wearing a jaunty, Dodger-blue beret and smoking a cigar. A pigeon with a blue head circles the old man's head and lands at his feet.

My mom comes up to me and hugs me. Then my father sneaks up behind her and starts tickling her. Then I tickle him, and my aunt tickles me, and soon all four of us are laughing and giggling.

When we calm down I look up. The old man and the pigeon have disappeared.

My father grabs my arm. He's serious now. He looks straight into my eyes. "Tap home plate and you'll find it," he says.

I jolted awake. All was silent and still. "Tap home plate and you'll find it." The Treasure!

After taking another quick look at the photos, as quietly as I could, I peeked out from behind the plywood. The coast was clear. I walked through the corridors toward the marble-floored rotunda that was the main entrance into the stadium. The night watchman, his head on his desk, was snoring away. Good. I tiptoed back, and found a door into the stands. I walked through it.

A nearly full moon lit up the field. The stadium was dark and the stands were deserted and weirdly quiet. Everything seemed beautiful in the moonlight in a strange, unearthly way.

I descended a stairway near the Dodger dugout and stepped onto the playing field. It was the same dirt and grass where Jackie and Pee Wee Reese and Duke Snider and Gil Hodges and all my other heroes ran and played. My skin prickled. Amazing.

I walked toward home plate. It didn't seem right to just

touch it with my finger. I fished a pencil out of my pack. I bent down and tapped the plate three times. On the third tap, a cloud obscured the moon and the ballpark got darker. It was eerie. Shivers ran up my spine.

Suddenly, a gnarled hand grabbed me hard on the shoulder. I started to scream but another hand closed around my mouth, choking off the sound.

Chapter 11

THE HAND WHIPPED ME AROUND. I was face to face with an elderly black man wearing a Dodger-blue beret. He was the same guy from my dream! The man hissed, "What the hell you doin' here?"

I opened my mouth and tried to speak but nothing would come out.

"What the matter with you, boy? I asked you a question."

"I...I...I don't know."

"You don't know what you doin' here?" His voice sounded like the gravel at the edge of the field. "That's the God's honest truth. I tell you this, you don't belong here. This ain't your home."

"I don't got a home."

"Oh ho. Don't got no home. Jeezus." He eyed me carefully. "Ain't safe to stay out here in the open too long. Not any more it ain't," he said less harshly, even though his fingers still dug into my shoulder.

A pigeon with a blue head swooped down and landed on the ground near us. The old man spoke to the bird. "It's okay. Go back home." The bird cocked its head, cooed once, and took off. We both watched it fly. It circled up to a nest in the roof high above the upper tier of seats near right field.

I had dreamed of that pigeon, too. This was so strange.

Once the pigeon landed in its nest, the man ordered, "Come with me." Limping slightly and muttering to himself, the old man kept a tight grip on the collar of my jacket as he slowly led me back under the stands. I wondered if I should try to jerk out of his grasp and run away, but even though he was old, his grip was strong.

The old timer took me down stairs and through winding corridors. At one particularly dark spot, he opened a trap door. Ushering me ahead of him, we both descended a long ladder. We emerged in a chamber lit by candles and lanterns.

I peered around, slack-jawed at the rustic but cozy room.

A fire burned in a fireplace cut from a 55-gallon drum. A bed, a couch, and a kitchen table with two chairs defined bedroom, living room, and kitchen. Colorful paintings adorned the walls and a partially-completed painting rested on an easel. Hundreds of books, neatly arranged in a large bookcase, covered one wall. Duke Ellington played on a battery-powered phonograph.

Completely bewildered, I started to ask, "What—?"

"First we eat, then we talk," the old man interrupted. "That's the civilized way of going about things." He removed a bunch of hot dogs from a fruit crate that served as a cupboard, and placed them on a piece of wire mesh that he set on some hooks inside the drum. As the hot dogs began to sizzle he took out rolls, sauerkraut, mustard, and relish, and placed these, along with two plates, on the table.

I walked around the room, looking at the paintings. "Did you paint these?"

"Not all of 'em." He turned the hot dogs. "That one there, that's a Charles Alston. And that one, that's Lois Mailou. You ever heard of them?"

Suddenly, the old man wheeled about, looking frantically around him, screaming, "Henry! Henry! What? What?"

I backed away from him, ready to bolt. My eyes were open wide.

But after a moment, he calmed down, breathing heavily. There was an awkward silence.

He used a dirty towel to lift the rack of hot dogs out of the fireplace. He placed it on the table. He forked two of the franks and put them on his plate. "Help yourself."

I sat down and put a couple of franks on my plate. I was about to take a bite, when the man interrupted me. "Gotta say grace first. Where's your manners?"

I put down my hot dog, a little embarrassed. "Sorry."

"Didn't your mama teach you that?"

"Don't have a mama," I told him.

The man regarded me closely. "Yeah, I remember you. I thought you was bigger, though."

"You know me?" *Huh? How could he know me?*

He didn't reply. He just bowed his head and half-spoke, half-sang the grace.

Bring me all of your dreams,
You dreamers,
Bring me all of your
Heart melodies
That I may wrap them
In a blue cloud-cloth
Away from the too-rough fingers
Of the world.

"Thank you, Lord. Amen."

"Amen," I said, too.

"That's Langston Hughes. Used to be a buddy of mine."

"It's nice," I said.

We ate silently for a while. The old man put down his fork. He looked at me and asked, "What's your name, anyway?"

"Eli Schwartz."

"They call me Henry. Henry Eugene Jenkins."

We shook hands across the table.

"Yeah, that's what they call me."

When we finished eating the dinner I took the box of Cracker Jacks out of my knapsack. "Mr. Jenkins, you want any Cracker Jacks? For dessert?

"Course I do," he said, almost indignant. "What kind of a man don't want Cracker Jacks?"

I handed the box to him. Henry chewed a few handfuls, then hummed a bit of "Take Me Out to the Ball Game." After a minute, he began singing, slowly and soulfully.

Take me out to the ball game,
Take me out with the crowd.

Buy me some peanuts and Cracker Jack.
I don't care if I never get back.
Let me root, root, root for the home team.
If they don't win it's a shame,
Cause it's one, two, three strikes you out
At the ol' ball game.

He sang, "you out," black style, instead of "you're out." I liked the way it sounded. I applauded. We sat without speaking for a while. Everything was quiet except for the flames licking around inside the 55-gallon drum-stove.

I broke the silence at last. "Where are we?"

"Look straight up. I'd say that's the pitcher's mound right up there."

"Really?"

"We're about twenty feet below. Cool in the summer. Warm in the fall. Now you tell me, what you doin' in Ebbets Field late at night?"

It didn't feel safe to mention the Treasure yet. I told Henry the next thing on my mind. "I'm not going to let him send me back to the Hole! I'd rather die first."

"Whoah. Back up a minute. Who you talkin' about?"

"Mr. Reiger." I said. "He owns the orphanage. I ran away."

"Where you goin' then?"

I pulled the photos from my coat pocket and handed them to Henry. "Look at this."

Henry examined them, then looked up. "Yeah?"

"It's my mother and father and me. In France. And that's my aunt. I'm gonna find her."

"Where she live?

"In Brooklyn somewhere. I think."

The old man shook his head. "Lot of people live in Brooklyn. What's her name?"

"Esther," I said.

"Just Esther?"

"I don't know her last name," I said. My face burned. What an idiot I was.

Henry passed the photos back to me. He stood up and took the plates to a washbasin.

I helped put things away.

"Well you can't stay here, that for dang sure," Henry said. "In two more days, this place become a ghost town."

"What will you do then?"

"Up top, I'm just an old crazy Negro. Down here, I can be myself, king of my world. Besides, the voices don't bother me so much down below."

"The voices?"

"Yeah," Henry continued. "I been livin' here and workin' here a long time."

"What kind of work do you do?"

"Oh, work on my projects. And night watchman, too, of course."

"What about that other man? The fat guy in the Rotunda."

"Old Coleman?" Henry said disdainfully. "He the number two guy. Well, maybe number one now. I'm semi-retired."

I helped dry the dishes. "How long you been living here?"

"How long? Since before it was Ebbets Field, that's how long."

"What do you mean?"

"Before this here place was a ballpark, it was a shanty town. Folks called it Pigtown."

"Why?"

"Why? Cause the pigs of course. Use your head, man."

"What pigs?"

"The pigs in Pigtown!"

"But what were they doing there?"

"In the middle of Pigtown," Henry said, "was a big, wide hole. Folks would throw their slops into that hole and farmers would bring their pigs there to eat. Look at this."

He led me to a section of wall covered with photos and paintings and drawings. He pointed to a painting that showed pigs snorting by the edge of a shallow pit. A large muddy field behind it was dotted with dilapidated shanties. Henry pointed at one of the shacks.

"That my house there. One day in 1908, this white man come by. Says we gotta move. Says a Mister Ebbets had bought all the properties in Pigtown. And now he gonna put up a ballpark." Henry paused for a moment, lost in the memory. "We didn't believe it. But we started believin' soon enough. They tore up the earth and began building the walls. At night, I'd sneak in, look all around." Henry gestured around the room. "And I discovered this cave kind of place, right below the ballfield."

One photo showed the brand-new Ebbets Field ready for opening day, banners draped along the outer walls and pennants flying from poles on the roof. People were arriving by foot and horse-drawn trolleys.

"I knew exactly where I could live," Henry continued. "Got me a job on the grounds crew. Made friends with all the night watchmen. Became watchman myself in 1934. Been here all that time. Never had no trouble. Until now."

I stared, mouth open, at the pictures. "Wow."

"Until now," Henry repeated.

"I know what you mean," I said.

Henry snorted. "Shoot. What do you know?"

"I mean about trouble. I heard these bad guys. They're planning to hurt Jackie. Tomorrow before the game. I tried to warn him, but I couldn't." It was a relief to tell a grown-up about the plan. Maybe he could help.

But Henry's reaction disappointed me. "Yeah? Jackie don't like no help from you or me or no one. He looks after hisself."

"These guys are really mean!"

"Jackie, he's faced a lot of meanness in his time. How you think he got all them white hairs at his age?"

"One of them isn't just after Jackie. He's looking for the Treasure." The words popped out of me.

Henry froze. "What!"

Since I had mentioned it, I figured I might as well continue. "Somewhere in Ebbets Field. Worth a million dollars. It gives you whatever you wish for."

Henry spat on the ground. "Bull."

"You heard about the Treasure?"

Henry poked in the fire irritably. "They got no right."

"I'm gonna try and find it myself."

The old man wheeled about to face me. "What the hell you talkin' about?"

"I'm gonna find the Treasure before they do. I'll find it and I'll be rich and I'll buy a big house near Coney Island, and my friend Kenny can come live with me. And I won't have to worry about that stupid Mr. Reiger or anything any more."

Henry's eyes flared. "You come bustin' in here where you ain't got no business! Trespassin'! Causin' trouble! You're just like them guys!"

"No I'm not. I—"

"Shut up!" Henry stomped about, limping, waving the fire poker in the air.

I backed away.

Flecks of spittle flew from Henry's mouth. He screamed, "Shut up and get the hell out of here! If I see you sneaking around here again, I'll have you arrested. So help me."

"But—"

"I said go!" He threw the poker down and it clanged onto the floor near my feet. Henry glared at me with wild eyes.

There was no telling what the crazy old man might do. I grabbed my pack and raced up the ladder.

Chapter 12

T HE NEXT MORNING I WAS BACK ON the street outside the
stadium. I had let myself out through an exit door
after spending the rest of the night behind my plywood
shelter. I had to risk leaving the park in order to warn
Jackie before the bad guys did something. It might be too
late if I waited until he entered the ballpark. After I
warned Jackie, I'd try to find Kenny. Then we could try
to sneak back into the park together and look for the
treasure.

I had a plan. Kenny and I would tuck in behind a large
family as they entered. When the father handed the ticket-
taker a handful of tickets for the whole family, we'd slip
through as two of the kids. If we got back in, I'd probably
be safe from Henry catching me because the park would
be so crowded with people.

I walked around the block to get warm and tried to think
of some way to warn Jackie. Maybe it'd be safe to tell a cop
out here on the outside. They couldn't all be crooked. On
the right field side of the stadium, several dozen fans were

clustered behind a police barricade. "What's going on?" I asked a kid who was waiting there.

"It's the player's entrance," he said. "I'm gonna get me an autograph."

"All the players come in this way?"

"Yup," he nodded. He pointed across the street to a small parking area marked, "Reserved." "That's where they park. They should start showing up soon."

Good. I'd wait there and hope Jackie came by.

A little while later, a car pulled in and someone got out. It was Carl Erskine, the Dodger pitcher.

"Ersk! Ersk!" people cried, reaching out toward him over the barricade.

He smiled and waved to the crowd, but he didn't come close or sign any autographs. A guard opened a door and he walked into the ballpark.

In another situation I would have been thrilled to see one of the Dodgers up close like this, but right now I was focused on warning Jackie of the danger he was in.

More and more fans crowded in behind the barricade, and a policeman arrived too. He stood on the street side of the barricade. *He's probably there to keep the fans under control.*

I ducked under the barricade and approached the cop. "Excuse me."

"Get behind the barrier, kid," the policeman barked.

"I heard these guys, they're gonna try to run over Jackie. They're—"

The cop ignored me and walked away. He motioned to the crowd. "Back up, folks."

Pee Wee Reese was now crossing the street.

"Pee Wee! Pee Wee!" the fans chanted.

Pee Wee acknowledged them with a doff of his hat as he walked past and entered the stadium.

I waited behind the barrier, my stomach tense, scanning the parking area and up and down the block.

A buzz passed through the crowd as a car pulled into the parking area across the street. "It's Jackie!" they shouted.

I noticed a second car slowly pull up to the curb about fifty yards down the street. It waited there, idling. I squinted at it. Was that Parton at the wheel?

Jackie Robinson climbed out of his car.

I strained at the barricade. "Jackie! Wait!" I screamed

But too many others were applauding, and yelling things like "Good luck, Jackie," and "We're with you," and they drowned me out.

Jackie stepped into the street.

The idling car pulled away from the curb and started driving fast up the street.

Several big teenagers muscled in front of me, blocking off my view.

I pushed my way through the teenagers, elbowing one of them in the ribs. I darted under the barricade into the street.

The cop looked up, startled. "Hey!" he yelled.

"Jackie! Wait!" I screamed again.

Jackie still didn't hear me. He continued walking forward. He was almost halfway across the street.

The cop yelled at me. "I told you to get back."

The car sped right toward Jackie.

Jackie smiled and waved to his fans, heedless of the danger. Finally, he glanced up at the car bearing down on him, and his smile vanished.

I dashed toward Jackie, made a leap, and tackled him. We fell off to the side, moments before the car screamed by and roared away up the street.

Jackie and I lay on the ground, my arms still around his hips. My chest heaved. My right leg hurt where I landed on it.

Photographers snapped pictures as a few people rushed to help us up.

The policeman squinted down the street toward the escaping vehicle.

A man wearing a press badge yelled, "Kid! Kid! Come over here."

In the midst of all the commotion, I looked up and noticed a woman standing quietly in the crowd staring at me. It was the female reporter I had spoken with the day before. Our eyes met.

Before I could say anything to her, Jackie put his arm over my shoulder. He looked shaken up. "Better come with me," he said in a quiet voice. "These newspaper guys are jackals." To the reporters who had somehow magically arrived on the scene and who were calling for a few words, Jackie said, "Not now, fellas."

He ushered me through the players' entrance away from the clamoring crowd. His arm felt heavy, strong. I leaned into it. I could have rested under it all day.

A little while later, Jackie and I sat by his locker. Other Dodgers were all around us. Some were joking, some of them quiet. A few looked at me curiously, but most simply ignored me. The room itself smelled moldy and was kind of dingy. But it was fantastic to be there, even though my body felt frozen stiff with shyness, to be sitting next to Jackie Robinson.

He smiled, though, and patted my back like he did to Pee Wee Reese after they made a double play, and this encouraged me to talk.

While he got dressed for the game I told Jackie the whole story of the plot to hurt him. "That's all I know, really," I concluded.

"Enough to save my life. The cops'll be on 'em now."

"Some of the cops were bribed."

"Most of them are honest," Jackie said. "Look, I gotta start getting ready for the game."

I stood up to leave. "Good luck today."

"Wait a sec. You want a ball?"

I nodded. What luck!

Jackie grabbed a brand new baseball from a box at the top of his locker. He spoke out loud as he wrote on the ball. "To Eli. Keep swinging. Your friend, Jackie Robinson." He handed me the white ball with the red lacing and the blue signature.

"Thanks!" I had never felt a new baseball before, and I loved its smoothness and the heft of it and the roughness of the stitching.

"And I can get you a pair of tickets for the rest of the Series," Jackie added.

"Great!" I shouted. I couldn't believe my good fortune. Now Kenny and I didn't have to sneak in.

I hesitated as Jackie laced up his cleats. Then I swallowed and asked him the question that was now foremost on my mind. "Jackie, do you know anything about the Treasure?"

He looked up, startled. "What'd you say?"

"You ever hear anything about the Treasure that's hid at Ebbets Field?"

Jackie stared at me a moment. "Old Henry's the one to ask about that."

"Henry Jenkins?"

He raised his eyebrows. "You know him?"

"I met him last night. He got really mad when I asked about the Treasure."

"You show him this ball," Jackie said, pointing at the ball that was still in my hands. "Then see what happens. Henry's a magic man."

Chapter 13

BEFORE I COULD GO LOOK FOR HENRY I had to track down Kenny. I couldn't wait to see the look on Kenny's face when I gave him his tickets and told him all about saving Jackie. But where was he? Had he gone back to the orphanage? Had he been taken back there by the cops? Was he out on the streets? I couldn't imagine him out there on his own. He must have gone back to the orphanage.

There was still an hour and a half before the game started. Enough time to take a trolley and sneak around and find Kenny if he was actually there. It was risky to go back, but I couldn't let Kenny be stuck in that dump when a seat was waiting for him at the World Series.

I got off the trolley a block from the orphanage. Seeing that dreary building again made my stomach hurt. It was lunchtime, so most everyone would be in the dining hall. I entered the alley, crept to one of the dingy windows, and stood on a milk crate so I could look in. The window was so dirty it was hard to see, but that also made it harder for anyone inside to see me.

Through a crack in the grime, I spotted the table where Kenny and I usually sat. James and Hank and Paul and Luis were there. No Kenny. James got up to empty his tray. The trashcan was near my window. As he dumped part of a soggy-looking sandwich into the garbage, I tapped on the window. He didn't hear me over the noise of the dining room. I tapped harder. This time, James looked up. His eyes got wide when he spotted me. I put my finger to my lips and motioned for him to meet me outside.

He looked all around, took his tray to the kitchen, and then darted out. In a minute, he was standing next to me in the alley. "What you doin' here, man? Reiger'll kill you if he finds you."

"I gotta talk to Kenny. Is he here?"

"He's in the Hole, man. Reiger slammed him in there for running away. And that's what he'll do to you, too, if he catches you."

"I gotta go to the Hole. I need to talk with Kenny."

"That's crazy," James said.

"Yeah, I know. Will you help me?"

James stared at me a moment. Then he smiled. "Sure."

"Great," I said. "I need you to be a lookout. Tell me if Reiger or anyone else is coming down the stairs. That'll give me time to hide."

We snuck around the side of the house to the back, crouching down whenever we passed in front of windows. In the back was a slanted storm cellar door. We were in luck. It wasn't locked. I tiptoed down the rickety wooden stairs, brushing cobwebs away from my face and hair.

James was right behind me. The cellar had the clammy smell and dungeon-like feeling that reminded me of my time in the Hole. Poor Kenny, stuck in there right now.

James stationed himself by the stairs to the kitchen, ready to warn me if anyone started to come down.

"Kenny!" I hissed by the door of the Hole.

"Eli?" He sounded like he couldn't believe his ears. "Is that you?"

"Yeah, you all right in there?"

"Not so good." His voice sounded weak, jittery. "Reiger said he'd let me out tomorrow. I'm just trying to take it minute by minute."

"Where's the skeleton key?" I had never gotten it back from Kenny after he got me out of the Hole.

"Oh, Eli. Reiger found out that was how we sprung you. He took it away from me."

"Shoot," I swore. "Kenny, I got us tickets for the Series! Don't have time to tell you about it now. But look, I'm going to put your tickets under the door. When you get out of the Hole, run away again and find me in Ebbets Field, okay?"

"You're joking, right?"

I took four tickets out of my pocket, one for each possible remaining game, if the Series went to seven games. Carefully, I slid them under the crack of the door to the Hole. There was just enough space for them to fit under.

"Feel by the door," I said. I knew it was so dark in the Hole, he wouldn't be able to see the tickets. "You got 'em?"

I heard his hand groping on the other side of the door. Then he cried out. "Yeah, I got something. I can't see it. I don't know what it is, but I got something."

"And now here's my money for Domingo." I slid a

bunch of coins under the doorway, almost the rest of the change I had scavenged after the game yesterday. "Pay him for me, okay."

"Sure," Kenny said.

James hissed, "Someone's coming, man. Scram!"

Chapter 14

THERE WAS NO TIME TO SAY ANYTHING more to Kenny. I sprinted to the storm cellar stairs.

Reiger bellowed at James, "What the hell are you doing here?"

"I was just seeing if Kenny was all right," James said, as I slipped out the storm cellar doors into the fresh air and sunlight. I hoped James wouldn't get in too much trouble for helping us.

I ran to the trolley stop and jumped on board as a trolley was taking off. How great it was to be free again. How great it was to be heading to Ebbets Field to watch the Dodgers in the World Series. How great it was to be looking for the Treasure. The only thing that would have made it better was if Kenny was with me.

At the park, I gave the guy my ticket and found my seat. It was close to the field behind third base. There was still a little time before the game would start, so I decided to walk around and look for Henry.

"Hey Esther!" a woman called out.

I wheeled about. But this Esther, hugging her friend hello, was a large black lady, not my aunt. I sighed and continued searching for Henry.

Someone tapped me on the shoulder, and I jumped. But it wasn't the bad guys or cops, only the female reporter.

"Sorry to scare you. I've been looking all over for you. That was really something, what you did before for Jackie."

I looked at my feet, my face growing warm.

"Really, it was very brave," she insisted.

"Thanks."

"Can I buy you a frank?" she asked.

"Okay." All of a sudden, I realized how hungry I was.

The Sym-Phony started playing "Roll Out the Barrel" as we made our way toward the hot dog stand. She told me her name was Betty and she worked for the *Herald Tribune*. She asked me to tell her my story. She was so pretty and seemed so nice. I had never talked to a friendly woman before. I told her how I ran away from the orphanage and all about the plot against Jackie.

At the hot dog stand, she took notes on her reporter's pad. When I finished my account, she put down her pencil and stared at me. "Drugs, gambling, assault, maybe even attempted murder. Jesus."

I nodded and took a bite of hot dog. Oh wow. It was so good. I closed my eyes for a second, savoring the taste.

Her eyes shone. "What a story! This beats writing about what color dress Mrs. O'Malley was wearing today, I'll tell you that." She suddenly looked worried. "My boss'll probably kill me."

"You think they'll try to get Jackie again?" I asked.

"I doubt it. It was stupid enough the first time." She studied me with concern. "You sure you're okay for tonight? Where are you gonna stay?"

I nodded. "I'm fine. I take care of myself now." I almost believed my own words.

Betty looked skeptical and stared at me closely for a long time. I thought she might turn me in, "for my own good" of course, but all she did was hand me her business card. "Well, call me if you need anything," she said. "Or if you overhear any more nasty plans, okay?"

I put the card into my coat pocket. As I took my hand back out of my pocket, the photo of my aunt and mother fell to the ground. Betty picked up the photo and looked at it.

"Who's this?" she asked.

"Oh. That's my mom and my aunt. In France. Before the war."

"They're beautiful," Betty said.

"I'm gonna find my aunt," I said. "She's the one on the right. Esther's her name. I think she might live in Brooklyn somewhere."

Betty gazed at the photo. Then she seemed to get an idea and smiled at me. "Can I borrow this? I'll get it back to you tomorrow."

"Uh, I don't know."

"I promise."

"Okay." I shrugged. I didn't really want to give away the precious photo, but I had a feeling it was the right thing to do. I liked Betty and trusted that she would get it back to me like she said.

By the bottom of the fifth inning, the Dodgers were

ahead four to three. I was feeding peanuts to a couple of pigeons in the aisle. Suddenly, Henry appeared directly next to me. Startled, I dropped the bag of peanuts.

"I'm sorry about last—" I began.

"You a strange one, all right."

I took the ball out of my pack and handed it to Henry. "Jackie said to show you this."

Henry examined the ball. He gave it back to me, then looked up and examined me. "Yeah, I thought so. You the one. No doubt about it now. You really are the one."

What's he talking about?

Henry continued. "I told him, 'It can't be him. You mistaken....Oh yeah, well I don't believe it...He just a kid...I don't care. Look, it make no nevermind to me he black or white. But a little boy? Come on. Too dangerous. Too hard.' Yeah, that's what I told him."

"Told who? Jackie?"

"'I know, I know,' I told him," Henry said. "'I remember those dreams. Yeah, he's an orphan. Yeah, he showed up like in the dream. I still don't believe it.' And I didn't until I seen you save Jackie this mornin'. This ball clinches it."

"You saw me?" I said. I hadn't noticed him.

"Saved his life."

"Nobody would listen to me."

"That 'cause you had to do it yourself."

"I guess," I said.

"Now, you gotta save something else," Henry said.

"What?"

Henry looked me right in the eye. "The Heart of Brooklyn."

"The Heart of Brooklyn?" *What in the world was that?*

70

Jackie said Henry was "a magic man." Was the Heart of Brooklyn some kind of magical object?

All he said was, "Be at my place tonight."

Just then, there was a loud crack of the bat. The crowd roared. I turned my head to see the ball sail over the fence. Duke Snider had hit a home run with two men on base. I jumped up and down screaming along with everyone. The Dodgers were going to win again! The series would be tied at two games each.

When I turned back, Henry had disappeared. The pigeon with a blue head was at my feet, pecking at the spilled peanuts.

Chapter 15

THAT NIGHT, I FOUND MYSELF IN Henry's underground home once again. We warmed ourselves by the glowing coals in the fifty-five gallon drum. A single kerosene lantern added the only other light to the cozy, art-filled chamber. I thought about Kenny, stuck in the Hole, and wished he could be there with me and meet Henry and see his cool home under the field.

Henry gazed at the shadows the fire made on the ceiling. "One night back in Pigtown, I was walking around, you know, explorin'-like. There was a full moon just like tonight. I saw something up in this one oak tree they hadn't cut down yet when they was buildin' the ball park." His eyes sparkled in the light from the embers. "Something was glinting in the moonlight. High up in a bird's nest. I climbed up. Lord Almighty, I couldn't believe my eyes."

"What?"

"Treasure, Eli."

"The Treasure!" I whispered. A thrill ran up my spine.

Henry knew all about it! Maybe he even still had it. Maybe he would share some of the money with me! Maybe I could live with him.

"Right from the start, I loved it. I knew I could never sell it."

"But you could've been rich! Did you wish for anything? You could have gotten anything you wished for."

"I was rich," Henry replied. "I had the Treasure. What else did I need?"

"But what good did it do you?"

"What good did it do me? Don't be a fool. The question is what good did I do it."

"What do you mean? It's not like it's alive."

"Not like it's alive!" Henry bellowed. "I told you. It's the Heart of Brooklyn."

"I don't even know what that means," I muttered.

Henry poked at the fire. "It means that all the hopes, all the dreams of all the people in Brooklyn, White and Colored and Jews and Christians and trees and rocks and birds and dogs and everyone, they all contained in that Treasure."

"That's craz—" I began. I caught myself before the full word came out, but the damage had been done.

"Crazy?" Henry hissed. "I'll tell you what's crazy. Crazy is killing yourself to make money and tearing up the earth and cutting down trees and making people slaves to factories and jobs and wearing a tie everyday and talking down to people like me. And like you, too, don't forget that. To them, you just a good for nothin' orphan. To them, I'm just a crazy old Negro. They don't know I been keeping it alive all these years. All these years, keeping the Heart of Brooklyn alive."

He paused for breath. "They don't understand." Henry limped back and forth. "Sell it, you asked me? Would you sell your own heart?" He glared at me.

I looked down at the ground, my face hot.

"Why you think the Dodgers so popular all these years? Even when they was losing all the time? Even when everyone called them bums?"

I shook my head. I had no idea.

"Because of the Treasure, that's why."

"But how could a thing —" I began.

"It's not a thing. I keep trying to tell you."

"The Treasure, then. How could the Treasure —"

"Magic," Henry said. "That's how. Come on." He beckoned for me to follow him.

We climbed up the ladder and made our way through the dark corridors and finally emerged onto the baseball field through a door in the stands behind home plate. The door closed behind us to blend in smoothly with the wall.

"I never noticed that door there before," I said, looking back at the wall.

"Lots of things you ain't never noticed."

The full moon began to rise above the edge of the stadium walls, casting shadows over the field. "Every full moon for the past forty-three years," Henry said, "I take the Treasure on a run around the bases. To recharge it." He shook his head ruefully. "Problem is, lately been getting harder and harder for me to do it. I'm too old. That's where you come in."

"What do you mean?"

"You the next guy. You the next Henry. I thought maybe it would be Jackie, but it ain't. You and he the only ones I ever told about it."

"How'd the rumors start, then? We even heard about it at the orphanage."

"One time, when Jackie and I was talkin' about the Treasure," Henry said, "somebody must've been lurkin' about in the shadows. Heard part of what I was sayin'."

"Is it true that if you stand with the Treasure on home plate in the moonlight, you get your wish?"

"That's what some people say," Henry replied. "Ready? The moon, she's rising quick."

The sky was brightening over the right field wall. I turned back to Henry. "You mean just run the bases with the Treasure?"

"I sure as hell don't mean taking it for a ride on the subway." Henry looked at my hands. They were trembling. "Don't worry. Pretend you hit a home run. Then, when you get to home, stand with it on the plate and wait for the moonlight to hit it."

"Then what happens?"

"You'll see. Here." Out of his beat-up old overcoat, Henry pulled out a weather-beaten wooden cigar box, tied round with red string. He handed it to me.

My whole body tingled, and for a second I felt like I was flying. "It doesn't weigh much," I said. "Can I open it? To see the — "

"No! Don't open it!"

"But I want to see it."

"Some things ain't meant to be looked at."

Maybe I couldn't look at it, but it could still give me my wish. This was my chance!

Henry gazed at the eastern sky. The moonlight was getting brighter by the minute. "Get going now. Not too fast, not too slow. Just right."

I began jogging toward first base, holding the box under my arm. Henry retreated back to the wall behind home plate. If Kenny could see me now, actually running the bases at Ebbets Field. Amazing.

I reached first base. I looked back and could barely make out the old man in the shadows, waving me on. I continued to second and then to third. I imagined the sounds of fans cheering and chanting my name. Eli! Eli! Eli! For a moment, I had a vision of my father, standing among the crowd, beaming at me.

The vision faded. With each step toward home, I was closer to making my wish. I rounded third and picked up speed and stepped triumphantly on home plate.

Henry was nowhere in sight.

The moon was now glowing over the rim of the right field wall and its light was about five feet from shining on the plate.

I stood there, facing the moon, holding the box out toward the light. As the moon rose higher above the stadium, its light crept closer to the box. Soon I would state my wish and the magic would make me rich.

Just as the moonbeams were almost to home, a figure burst through a door on the first base side of the stands. It was Parton, the thug who had tried to run over Jackie! "Over there!" he yelled, his words echoing through the empty stadium.

Chapter 16

PARTON RACED DOWN THE STEPS TOWARD THE FIELD.
Charlie came limping behind him.

In a panic, I looked around for Henry, but the old man had disappeared. I tensed to run, but then hesitated. The moonlight was almost shining on the box. I needed my wish.

Parton and Charlie ran down to the bottom of the stands.

I urged the moon to hurry up and reach home plate. "Come on. Come on."

Parton vaulted the railing and landed on the field behind first base. Charlie was close behind.

Finally the moonbeams hit the old cigar box. I spoke as fast as I could. "I wish for a million dollars." As soon as the words were uttered, I turned and ran toward the visiting team's dugout near third base.

A whistle rang out from somewhere in the shadows near the foot of the stands. Then, from the eaves and rafters of the stadium, came a flapping and a squawking that grew louder and louder.

Hundreds of pigeons soared down toward Parton and Charlie. The birds flapped in their faces and buzzed their heads, delaying the two men as they ducked and tried to bat the pigeons away.

I leapt into the dugout, knocking baseball bats and practice balls onto the floor behind me. Maybe that would slow them down. At the back of the dugout, I opened a door and ran through it. As I raced down a dark corridor, I heard a crash and swearing and a second crash. I imagined Parton and then Charlie tripping on the balls and bats.

I paused, uncertain, when I reached an intersection where the corridor forked.

"Pshht!" came a sharp whisper. Henry was almost directly above me, lying flat on a narrow shelf near the ceiling. "Climb up." he whispered. "There." He pointed at a few wooden crates, set out to form a crude staircase.

The thugs' footsteps were coming closer down the hallway.

I climbed up the crates and flattened myself onto the shelf near Henry.

Charlie and Parton ran right below us and paused at the intersection. "Go that way," Parton ordered. "Don't lose him."

Parton ran down one of the corridors. Charlie stood still and listened. "Got to find it," he muttered. He took off down the other corridor.

When their footsteps had faded away, Henry and I sat up.

"I'm a fool," Henry whispered.

"I'm sorry, Henry."

"Didn't think they were this close."

"The moonlight hit the box," I said. "That's good, isn't it?"

Henry grumbled something I couldn't make out.

"You think I'll get my wish?"

Henry merely folded his arms around his shoulders, ducked his head, and rocked back and forth in silence.

After a while, we sensed that the coast was clear. We climbed down and made our way to Henry's home. When we descended the ladder into Henry's apartment all we could do was stare. The place had been ransacked. The bed was overturned and the mattress slashed. The couch lay on its side, its cushions also slashed. The bookshelf had been toppled and books were strewn across the floor. Paintings, removed from the walls, lay on the floor. Some had been torn or trampled on.

"AHHHH!" With a roar, Henry picked up a chair and hurled it against the wall.

I placed the box with the Treasure on the kitchen table. I righted the bookcase and started to put books back in it.

"Leave it be," Henry commanded.

"But Henry —"

"I said leave it be!"

I sat on the remaining chair, as Henry stomped around, kicking books and cursing.

He finally quieted down and he stood looking all around, his chest heaving.

"What do we do now?" I asked.

"I knew it was time," Henry said. "Just didn't want to believe it."

"I'm sorry."

"I shoulda known. You come here not to be the new guy, but to help me return it."

"What do you mean 'return it'?"

"If the Treasure falls into the wrong hands, it'd be disaster. Better for it to disappear than for that to happen."

"But why?"

"That Treasure more powerful than you know. Bad guys get it, they get hold of the hopes and dreams of all the people. Hopes and dreams is the greatest power in the world. Bad guys would surely abuse power like that, use it to manipulate people, to force them to do things. The wrong people get the Treasure, who knows what might happen? Could be like Nazi days in Brooklyn."

I imagined armed soldiers in black uniforms forcing men, women, and children to enter a horrible factory belching black smoke.

"Could be like slavery." In my mind's eye, I saw men, women, and children chained together at the ankles and forced to shovel coal into the furnaces. A child looked up at me with lost, desolate eyes. The look of despair and hopelessness.

Henry's eyes were closed as he spoke. "Without dreams, without hope, the people would have nothing. Happiness would disappear. Their own hearts would harden."

I shuddered.

Henry opened his eyes. "No, we can't let that happen. We gotta return it." He sighed. "It means the end of the Brooklyn Dodgers, though."

I stared at the old man. "The end of the Dodgers?"

"They can't continue without the Treasure. It's too much a part of them."

"That's not fair!" I shouted. "It can't be!"

Henry was calm and resigned now. "Tomorrow morning, I gotta do a few things. Meet me out in the left field stands during the game."

I started to cry.

Henry put his arm around my shoulders. "Don't you worry, Eli. My grandma always used to say, 'The day time's wiser than the night time.' You'll see."

Chapter 17

The next day, the stands were packed once again. It was a sunny October afternoon. The fans were in a good mood and lustily cheered every pitch. I stood alone in a relatively hidden corner of the left field stands. I looked anxiously around, one eye on the field and one eye searching for Henry.

Nearby, someone had a portable radio that was broadcasting the play by play. It was strange to watch the game live and then hear it described on the radio a fraction of a second later.

"Berra swings and misses," the radio croaked. "Strike two. Dodgers holding onto a four to one lead here in the top of the sixth. Yogi hits a high fly to left. Gilliam gathers it in easily. Two away."

"Dang, Henry," I said to myself. "Where are you?"

Looking around the stands, I did a doubletake. There was Kenny! "Hey Kenny," I yelled.

He ran up to me, flushed and out of breath.

We hugged. "You don't know how glad I am to see you," I said. "What happened? How'd you get out?"

"Well, I ran from that guard who was chasing us and slipped back out onto the street. Then, I couldn't figure out another way to get back into the ballpark. Plus I was afraid that guy would see me and catch me. I was getting really hungry, so I went back to the orphanage. Man, Reiger was furious with me. He wanted to know where you were, but I wouldn't tell him. The jerk made me stay in the Hole for two days."

"Wow, I'm sorry," I said. "Thanks for not squealing on me."

"Of course. I only wish I'd been able to listen to yesterday's game. I thought about you here watching it. They let me out of the Hole this morning. I gave the money to Domingo, and then I slipped away as soon as I could." He looked all around, his eyes wide. "I can't believe I'm in Ebbets Field!"

"Yeah, I know what you mean," I said. "It's like a dream."

We both stared at the action down on the field for a while. The Dodgers got the third out and trotted off the field. The Yankees came on.

Kenny turned back to me. "Hey, how does it feel to be famous?"

"What're you talking about?"

"Didn't you see this?" Kenny fished out from his back pocket a copy of *The New York Post.*

A photo on the back page showed Jackie Robinson with his arm around my shoulder. The headline read, "ORPHAN SAVES ROBINSON, SEARCHES FOR AUNT."

Reproduced next to it was the photo of my mother and my aunt in France.

"Uh oh," I said, "Reiger will know where to find me now."

"I overheard him talking to Mrs. Reiger. He said he was going to track you down and make sure you didn't blab. Take care of you once and for all."

I flinched. "I thought it was bad enough just to have those goons after me." I glanced nervously around the stadium, then back at Kenny. "Good thing you found me before Reiger did. Now I need to find somebody. His name is Henry."

"Who's Henry?"

"He protects the Treasure. He's a little crazy." I told Kenny all about the plot to injure Jackie and how I met Henry, and Charlie and those guys looking for the Treasure.

His jaw fell open. "Wow. But you know, now that your picture's been in the paper and all, those goons might be looking for you again."

"Great. Them *and* Reiger. Come on. Let's look for Henry. He'll know what to do."

By the bottom of the seventh inning we still hadn't located the old man. Kenny and I peeked out from behind a pillar. I had to be careful that Charlie and Parton didn't spot me.

"Is that him?" Kenny pointed to an elderly black man sitting nearby.

"No. Henry always wears a blue beret."

A few minutes later, Kenny nudged me. "There's an old black guy with a blue beret."

"Where?"

Kenny pointed toward the bleachers.

"That's him!" I shouted. "Come on."

Kenny paused. "I think just you should go. He sounds like he might be kind of skittish around new people."

"Good thinking," I said. "Wait here, okay?"

Keeping an eye out for Charlie and Parton, I trotted toward Henry. When I got to the end of his row I saw that the old man was not watching the game. His eyes were closed and he was rocking back and forth, muttering to himself. The people on either side of him eyed him warily.

I called out down the row, over the noise of the crowd. "Henry!"

Henry kept rocking and muttering.

"Excuse me. Excuse me." I made my way down the row closer toward Henry, squeezing past the other people. I tugged his sleeve. "Henry," I said gently.

His eyes jerked open. At first, he didn't seem to recognize me. Then, a smile grew across his face. "Yeah, I remember you."

"Henry. Listen. What about You-Know-What? What are we going to do?"

Henry's eyes cleared, and he seemed sane once more. "Can't talk here."

We moved to a more private spot behind a pillar. The stands erupted with applause and shouts as the game unfolded on the field below us.

"Didn't want to remember," Henry said sadly. "Just enjoying the game like it was any other day. Not the day when the Treasure goes away."

"How long will it be gone?" I asked.

"No way to know."

We both turned to watch a man in the stands behind us make a good catch on a foul ball. "Jackie gotta see the box before it goes," Henry said.

"Why?"

"Jackie's part of the magic. Never would have played in the Majors if not for the Treasure. He'd want to see it one last time. Show Jackie the box and then bring it back to me."

"It's too dangerous. Those guys are probably looking for us. Plus the orphanage owner is hunting me, too."

Henry was firm. "Jackie would want to see it." From beneath his overcoat, Henry removed the old wooden cigar box wrapped with red string. I took the box and put it into my pack. My body tingled again like it did when I held the Treasure the first time.

"When I get back, what are we gonna do?"

Henry had started to sing, and didn't answer my question. Or maybe he did and I just didn't understand at the time. "*Buy me some peanuts and Cracker Jack. I don't care if I never get back.*"

"Henry?"

Henry merely walked away, still singing. "*Cause it one, two, three strike you out at the ol' ball game.*"

I stared at him. He sure could be exasperating. I wanted to look in the box really bad. To at least get a glimpse of the Treasure before it went away, but Henry told me not to, and maybe if I did look, I wouldn't get my wish. Plus now, the most important thing was to keep it away from the bad guys.

I trotted back to where Kenny was waiting. "Now I have to find Jackie," I told him.

Kenny looked puzzled.

"I'll tell you later. Meet me back here."

"Be careful," Kenny warned.

It seemed to me too late for that.

Chapter 18

JACKIE ROBINSON WAS AT BAT.

Fans called out encouragement. "You get him, Jackie."

"Home run now."

"Let's go, Jackie."

I ran down the steps toward the field, pausing to watch Jackie swing and miss. Then I froze. Charlie and Joan were walking directly toward me. Charlie's eyes grew wide when he spotted me. He said something to Joan and pointed at me.

I turned to escape and ran smack into Parton! I dodged out of his grasp and ran back up the aisle. A fat woman was lumbering up the steps, blocking my way. Parton's thick hand grabbed the back of my pack. But then he slipped on part of a hot dog on the ground and tumbled to the side.

I slipped out of Parton's grasp, darted around the fat lady, and dodged in and out of the spectators and vendors. Charlie and Joan had a harder time than me making their way through the crowded aisles, and I gradually pulled away from them.

Once more I stopped short. The dapper guy in the brown suit and derby hat who I had seen under the stands, the boss, was striding straight toward me. Behind me, Charlie and Joan were getting closer.

"Stop him!" Charlie yelled.

The boss smiled at me, a mean, cold smile.

I turned to run down the nearby steps, but there was Parton again. There were too many of them.

The goon lunged at me.

I pushed him backwards.

He lost his balance and fell down a couple of steps right into a hot-dog cart. A big mustard jar slid off the cart and crashed onto him. Its top came off and soaked Parton in mustard.

He swore as I started to run away. But the boss was too quick. He caught me by the collar.

"Running off so soon?" he hissed. "We have some business to discuss." His voice was like ice.

"Let me go!" I cried. "You were going to kill Jackie." I turned to the spectators near us. "He's a crook! He's a crook!"

"Shut up," he ordered.

"Crook!" I screamed.

He slapped me hard across the face.

I felt tears start to come, and willed them back down.

A tall man wearing a fedora yelled, "Leave the kid alone."

"Mind your own stinkin' business," the boss snapped back.

"Help!" I yelled, but no one seemed to hear me over the noise of the crowd.

The boss cinched my collar, choking me and cutting off any further yelling.

Charlie ran up to us. "What're you doing here?" he said to the boss.

"Somebody's got to get things done here. It's obvious I can't depend on you guys."

Parton joined us, rubbing his shin and wiping mustard from his hair and clothes.

People in the stands yelled for our group to shut up and get out of the way.

"Bring the kid downstairs," the boss ordered.

With Charlie clasping me on one side and Parton on the other, they dragged me through a door and down below the stands. Parton stunk of mustard.

They took me to the room under the stands where I first overheard them making their plans. My belly cramped. Was my life over? There was no telling what they might do to me. Charlie and Parton and the boss surrounded me. I didn't see Joan. Above us, from time to time we heard a muffled roar from the stands.

"So the kid here foiled our plan. Big deal. We can make other arrangements," the boss said. "What makes him so interesting that you'd chase him all around Ebbets Field? That's what I want to know."

"The little twit knows about the Treasure," Parton blurted out.

Charlie gave Parton a dirty look. "You idiot."

"Of course." The boss chuckled. "The Treasure. I heard you were interested in it, Charlie. I'll need a cut, you know that. A major cut."

"See," Charlie said to Parton.

"If there really *is* a treasure," the boss added.

I tried to dart between the boss and Parton, but Parton leaned in and squashed me against the boss.

"Keep him under control," the boss ordered.

Parton jerked my arm painfully behind my back. "Where is it? Where's the old man?"

I gasped. "I don't know."

"He's lying," the boss said.

Parton tightened the arm hold. My arm felt like it might break.

"What did you say?" Parton asked again. I could tell he was enjoying this. He yanked on my arm again, harder this time.

I yelped.

"Ease up, Parton," Charlie said. "He's just a kid."

"Yeah, a kid who might have his hands on a million bucks."

Charlie's eyes lit up. "What you got in your pack there, kid?"

I squirmed under Parton's grip.

"Didn't occur to me the twerp might have it on him," Charlie said. He searched through my pack and pulled out the box.

Parton whistled. "Well, lookee here."

"Bingo," Charlie said. Charlie took out his switchblade. His hand trembled a little as he cut the string around the box.

"No! Don't open it!" I yelled. I closed my eyes and braced myself for an explosion or a genie or some other magical reaction when the box opened. But nothing happened. I opened my eyes.

Charlie's face fell. The box was empty. "You little thief!" he screamed. He shook me hard. "Where is it?"

My brain felt all jangled. I couldn't think straight. "I don't know."

"Maybe there's a map or something hidden in it," Parton said.

Charlie searched the box more thoroughly. He threw it onto the ground.

Parton swore.

"The old man's playing the kid for a fool," Charlie spat out. "Playing all of us for fools."

Suddenly, everything became clear to me. I felt my insides go numb. My heart went cold. "There's no Treasure. He's crazy, that's all." *Now, I wouldn't get a million dollars. I was an idiot. I was a broke and homeless idiot.*

At that moment, Joan entered, dragging Henry along with her. Henry was giggling and talking to himself, and did appear to be quite crazy.

"Well, well, well," Parton said. "Speak of the devil."

"He says he'll talk," Joan said.

The boss stared at Henry. "Let's get down to business. Where is it?"

Henry giggled. "Right here, of course. Where else would it be?"

Parton let go of me and walked up to Henry. His bulk towered over Henry. "Don't play games with us, old man."

"I ain't playing no games. You the one be playin' games."

Parton grabbed Henry's coat and raised his hand to strike Henry. "You stupid —"

"Stop!" I yelled. "Stop! Can't you see? He's just an old man. A sick, crazy old man."

Everyone stared at me.

"And we're crazy for ever believing him. There's no Treasure. There never was a Treasure. There's no wishes. There's no magic. There's no million bucks. The whole thing's bull." I broke down sobbing.

Henry's smile disappeared. He stared at me, clear-eyed now. "That what you think, eh?"

I tried to stop crying, but I couldn't.

"Just like the rest after all," Henry said bitterly. He suddenly seemed weak and old. He shut his eyes and began rocking back and forth.

"He's still trying to trick us," Charlie said. He shook Henry until the old man's eyes opened. "Where is it?"

"Fools. All of you."

With a quick movement, Parton took out a knife and held it to my throat. "You don't tell us, the boy is dead." The steel bit into my skin.

My legs shook and I thought I might pass out.

Henry's eyes flashed. "All right, all right, I'll tell you. Just leave the boy alone."

"Good man," the boss said.

"The hall to the Dodgers' dugout," Henry began. "You'll see a fire extinguisher on the right. Right above it is a shelf near the ceiling. There's a bunch of boxes. Under the bottom one, that's where it is."

"Take us."

Henry tottered.

I tried to move toward him, but Parton still had hold of me.

Joan helped Henry sit on a crate. "He's too weak," she said.

"We'll check it ourselves, then," the boss said. "Charlie, you and Joan go see if the old man is telling the truth. And I'll go with you to keep you honest. Parton, you stay here and watch these two." He turned to Henry. "I hope you're telling the truth, old timer. For your sake."

The boss, Charlie, and Joan exited, leaving me and Henry under the guard of Parton. It was two against one. But a kid and a weak old man against a giant like Parton? It was hopeless.

Parton rubbed his sore shin. He winced. "I owe you for these, kid."

The crowd roared above us.

Henry stared at the floor, muttering to himself.

Parton paced, waiting.

While I was trying to think of what to do, I noticed a movement by the door. It was Kenny!

Parton saw him, too. The big man made a quick lunge and grabbed Kenny by the coat. He dragged him into the room. "What're you doing here?"

"I, uh—"

While Parton was distracted, I picked up a wooden crate lying nearby.

"I was looking for the bathroom," Kenny said.

"Get the hell—" Parton stopped in mid sentence as I smashed the crate over his head. The big man slumped slowly to the floor.

"Kenny!" I said.

He stared down at Parton. "Wow, good smash, Eli. I saw them catch you and followed you down here."

"Come on, Henry." I touched the old man's shoulder. "Let's get out of here. Are you strong enough?"

Henry pulled away. "Don't bother about me. I'm just a sick, crazy old man. Isn't that what you said? Run on now. Save your own behinds."

"Henry, I'm sorry. I didn't mean it like that."

"And I thought you was different. I thought you could see."

"But the box was empty," I said. "You tricked me."

Henry picked up the box, which was lying on the ground where Charlie threw it. "It's not empty. You just can't see anything."

"That doesn't make sense," I said.

"At first, I could see the Treasure. For a long time I could see it. A beautiful diamond, solid as this floor here." Henry tapped the floor with his foot. "After a while, though, it began to fade. I could look right through it, like peering through a mist. Then it faded and faded, and about seven years ago, it disappeared completely. But as it disappeared, the magic got stronger. That's how magic works."

Kenny's eyes grew wide. "Wow."

"But the Treasure's still there in the box. It's still there. You just can't see it. That's the only thing keeping it safe, but sooner or later, they'd figure it out. Then they'd have control of people's dreams. And everything would become a nightmare. Yeah, it has to be returned."

"But why'd you tell them to look under the stands?" I asked.

"Just a decoy to give your friend here time to show up."

"How did you know I w—"

Henry interrupted. "They'll be back soon. It's up to you, Eli."

"What do you mean?"

"You say you want money. I've hidden five hundred bucks right down the hall. I'll tell you where to find it. If you still think I'm crazy, then go now, take the money, and get on with your life. No hard feelings." Henry looked me in the eyes. "If you believe me, though, then you gotta help."

I hesitated. Five hundred dollars was a fortune. There were so many things that amount of cash could buy. A place to live. Food. Warm clothes. Books. New shoes.

I looked from Henry to Kenny. They both stared at me, waiting for my response.

There was no time to think it through. The boss and Charlie and Joan would return any minute.

Maybe Henry was crazy, but he was counting on me. Money or no money, I couldn't just leave him. Plus, the Heart of Brooklyn was part of my heart, too.

I swallowed. "I'll help. What do I need to do?"

Henry nodded. "That nest I found the Treasure in back in Pigtown? A long time ago, I placed it high up in the rafters. You gotta put the box back into the nest."

"Why?" Kenny asked.

"From there, my friend will take the Treasure away. Keep it safe until the next time it's supposed to show up."

"Where exactly is the nest?" My voice shook a little.

"In the upper level in right field, at the top of the roof-beams."

"How do I get up there?"

"How do you think? You climb."

"It's three stories up!"

"He's afraid of heights," Kenny explained. "I could do it."

"That's good of you to offer, son," Henry said. "But Eli's the one who has to do it. There's no other way."

I nodded, even though merely the idea of climbing so high almost paralyzed me. "I'll do it."

He handed the box to me. "Here."

It tingled in my hands like before. I stashed it back in my pack. Once it was gone I'd never feel that tingling again.

Angry voices were getting nearer. Reiger, Charlie, and Joan.

Parton groaned and stirred on the floor.

I started to tell Henry something. I wasn't sure exactly what I wanted to say. "Henry, I—"

Henry, though, turned to Kenny. "And you, go find Jackie. Tell him what happened and that Henry said, 'The time has come.'"

I didn't want to leave Henry alone. "But—"

The voices were getting louder.

"Go, go, go!" Henry ordered.

Kenny and I took off running.

Chapter 19

I RAN ALONG AN AISLE IN THE UPPER TIER of the right field stands, dodging empty beer cups and food wrappers. The scoreboard showed the top of the ninth with the Dodgers leading 5 to 3. The fans made a racket all around me. Normally, I'd be cheering like crazy with them, but now I couldn't afford to get distracted by the game.

I squinted at the pigeon's nest in the girders way above the seats, and my stomach lurched. I tottered a little with dizziness and grabbed a column to steady myself. *This is nuts. It's too high.* But I had to. Like in my dream back in the orphanage of batting for the Dodgers, all of Brooklyn was depending on me.

When I reached the back wall, I stared at a latticework of metal beams criss-crossing above me. Sweat dripped into my eyes. With a shaky hand, I wiped it away.

I checked to see if anyone was looking in my direction. Everyone around me was watching the action on the field. I took a deep breath and began climbing up the wall. The metal beams felt cold and damp. When I got about twenty feet up I hoisted myself up and inched out onto a long steel girder that ran parallel to the roof. I sat there for a minute, hoping my heart would stop pounding. It didn't.

The smell of beer and hot dogs and peanuts drifted up to me. Normally, I liked that smell, but right now it was sickening. I looked down three stories to the stands below. My head swam. My arms felt numb and my field of vision narrowed. To keep from pitching forward I gripped the beam tight with my legs.

A movement below me caught my eye. It was Charlie. He had entered the upper tier. My stomach clenched. He spoke to an usher. The usher pointed in the direction I had jogged.

Move, I told myself. *You have to move.* I looked along the girder. It ran at an angle up toward the pigeon's nest, which was near the apex of the roof, maybe ninety terrifying feet away. My eyes told me it was the same distance as from third base to home plate. My gut said different. It seemed miles away.

I straddled the girder and scooted myself forwards. The next time I looked down, I saw that Parton and Joan had joined Charlie. They were looking all around. My arms and legs trembled. I took a deep breath to try to steady myself, but it didn't help.

With shaking limbs, I inched along the beam. There was the nest about forty feet ahead now. It looked barely big enough for the box to fit into.

I gripped the beam more tightly with my legs and wiped my sweaty hands on the sleeves of my jacket. *Just a little more. Just a little bit more.* I continued sliding my way forward along the beam.

When I looked down again, Charlie and Parton were

standing almost directly below me. My hand brushed against a stray twig and knocked it off the girder. It fluttered down right at their feet. Charlie looked up. "There!" His voice carried up to me.

"Get him. Get *it*," Parton barked.

Charlie ran back to the wall and began climbing the ironwork. I pulled myself forward on the beam on my butt as fast as I could. But then I got stuck. I tried to move, but something was holding me back. What was going on? I felt behind me with my hand. My pants had gotten snagged on a bolt. I tugged hard and heard a ripping sound. Shoot! My pants were torn, but at least I could move again.

The stands erupted with a huge cheer. A quick glance toward the field showed that the Dodgers had made the final out and won the game. Gladys Gooding started playing the "Follow the Dodgers" theme song on the stadium organ. I paused to gather my energy.

Looking down, I saw that, no longer distracted by the game, people were pointing and staring up at me. Police rushed onto the scene. They cleared people out of the space directly under me.

I needed to get moving again, but I found that I couldn't. My arms and legs had gone numb. All strength had left them.

I looked over my shoulder. Charlie was gaining on me.

My head swam. Everything started spinning around me. I listed to the side!

My hands lost their grip, and I started tumbling toward the right. My left leg lifted off the beam, as my right leg and my torso dangled in the void beneath me.

Desperately, I lunged back with my left leg, and it barely caught hold. The edge of the girder bit into my leg. The rest of my body was turned sideways, parallel to the ground.

The sound of a hundred gasps of the people below drifted up.

My grip on the beam with my left leg began to slip. *This is it. It's over.* Strangely, all fear left me. My mind became empty, calm.

Time seemed to have stopped. In this field of stillness, I thought of Kenny and Henry and the Heart of Brooklyn. It couldn't end like this. I couldn't let go.

I gripped the beam with my left thigh and calf as tightly as I could. Slowly, slowly, I pulled my body back onto the girder. With a final grunt, I made it. I lay belly down on the cold metal, panting hard. The muscles of my stomach and my leg burned. *That was close!*

When I sat up, I knocked my Dodger cap loose. I made a grab for it, and almost fell off the beam once again. The hat drifted slowly to the seats far below. "Darn it." My lucky hat was gone. At least I was still alive. Now I had no choice but to continue, hat or no hat, luck or no luck. I crawled forward on hands and knees.

Charlie was a lot bigger and faster than me. I heard him grunting, and looked behind me. He was only about twenty feet away. "Give it up, kid."

The setting sun streamed low over the roofline of left field and shone directly onto the nest. This close, I saw that the beam I was on ended about five feet shy of the nest. I wouldn't be able to get right up to it. Shoot! Now what? I looked back. Charlie was getting steadily nearer.

Finally, I reached the end of the beam, as near to the nest as I could manage. There was no other choice than to try to throw the box into the nest from here. I stopped crawling, and straddled the beam with my legs. I took off my pack and pulled out the box. "Don't miss," I said out loud. My voice shook. I had to save the Heart of Brooklyn. Even if it meant the end of the Treasure for me personally.

"What're you doing?" Charlie screamed. "Stop!"

Hugging the beam tight with my legs, I took a deep breath.

I raised my hand.

I tossed the box toward the nest.

It seemed to float forever in the empty air. Then it landed on the edge of the nest, teetering there. Would it fall out and tumble down to the stands?

Time stood still once again.

I held my breath.

A slight breeze rustled my hair as it blew past me toward the nest. The wind tipped the box into the nest.

I breathed out. *I did it!*

At the very moment the box slipped into the nest, the sun disappeared below the edge of the stadium wall and the park suddenly seemed a lot darker.

A pigeon with a blue head swooped toward the nest. It alighted on the box and opened the lid with its beak. Then, it took off, its claws seeming to hold an invisible object. It circled away above the playing field.

A strange, flapping sound filled the stadium. Hundreds and hundreds of pigeons flew out of their nests and gathered into a huge spiraling flock. Then, led by the blue-headed pigeon, the flock circled the bases, flying over first and second and then third base. When they got above home plate, they began to ascend. Higher and higher they rose in circles, until they were above the roofline. They took off, heading west toward the darkening sky. And then they were gone.

Chapter 20

THE STADIUM WAS STILL. The people were silent. Down below, I noticed that several women, and even some men, wept. The breeze picked up and stirred the trash on the floor of the aisles and rows. The sun sank below the horizon. I think we all felt a strange, melancholy, beautiful feeling.

I watched the pigeons disappear into the sky. I looked back at the nest. The box rested there, its lid off, truly empty now.

Gradually, the people below started talking quietly to each other.

Charlie called out to me. I looked back, and we gazed at each other. His eyes were wide. "What just happened?"

I smiled at him. "Magic."

The spectators below watched me and Charlie turn around on the beam and climb back down. It was easier going down. I was too worn out to panic. When I finally touched ground, several cops were waiting for me. But so was Reiger!

Photographers and reporters shouted questions at me.

Reiger elbowed his way through the crowd. "Thank God, the boy's all right. If you please, gentlemen, now is not the time for questions. You can see he's quite disturbed." He put his arm around my shoulders and tried ushering me away from the crowd. "Come on, son, you've been through a lot."

I jerked out of his grasp. "That was the Treasure," I yelled to the bystanders. "It's gone now. Don't you understand?"

"There, there, son. It's okay now. It's all over. No one's gonna hurt you," Reiger cooed. His voice filled me with ice.

"They were trying to steal it but they can't now. It was magic. You saw it. Didn't you?"

The crowd murmured. I think they were not sure what they had seen.

"I'm this boy's guardian," Reiger said. "He's a very troubled young man. Please, no questions. I'll take him home now." He grabbed my arm, more firmly this time, and started leading me away.

The Boss emerged from the crowd and grabbed my other arm. "Hey, Reiger. Looks like we have something in common."

Reiger looked surprised, but smiled. "Small world."

I jerked my arm but couldn't break free. "Let me go! They're liars! They're liars!" I screamed. I nodded toward the boss. "This one tried to kill Jackie." I nodded toward Reiger. "And this one beats up little kids." No one seemed to recognize me from the paper. Fear gripped my belly once again.

"The child's very agitated," the boss said. He continued dragging me away. The crowd parted to let us pass.

Reiger and the boss pulled up short when Charlie suddenly blocked their way. "Let the kid go. Both of you."

My mouth fell open. Charlie was helping me?

"Get lost, Charlie," Reiger said.

"Get out of my way, Charlie, or so help me-" the boss added.

"So help you what?"

"I don't listen to junkies like you," the boss said. Despite his bravado, he seemed to me to be scared. But he still kept a tight grip on my arm.

"You're gonna listen this time. Let go of the kid."

The boss spat at Charlie's feet. "The hell with you." He tried to push past Charlie, dragging me alongside him.

Charlie reared back and socked the boss in the jaw.

The boss stumbled back, dazed.

I slipped out of his grasp.

Reiger started to run away, but Charlie caught him and decked him, too.

Some people whispered, "It's Jackie!" The crowd parted, and Jackie Robinson, still in his baseball uniform, walked up, accompanied by Betty, the reporter, and two policemen.

Kenny was right behind them. Further back, Joan and Parton were in handcuffs.

I ran to Jackie. He put his arm around me. "You okay, son?"

I nodded. His arm was so strong. He looked up toward the girders. "Good job up there. Sure was courageous of you."

Charlie tried to disappear into the crowd, but a cop nabbed him.

As the police handcuffed the boss, Reiger, and Charlie, Betty rushed up to me and hugged me. "I got promoted!"

The crowd parted to let the policemen lead the boss, Reiger, and Charlie away.

I called to Charlie as he walked past me. "Thanks, Charlie. I'm sorry you gotta go to jail again."

Charlie smiled. "Take care of yourself, kid." He turned to the boss and smirked. "I'll see you in Sing Sing."

The boss glared at me as he was led off. I held his gaze, and he looked away.

Reiger spat at my feet as the cops ushered him away, too.

Kenny ran up to me with my Dodger cap in his hand! "Got your lucky cap for you, Eli."

I grinned and put my cap back on my head, surrounded by Jackie and Betty and Kenny, as flashbulbs flashed.

Suddenly, I remembered Henry. I looked around and saw the old man slumped on a chair nearby, looking utterly spent.

Henry sat up a little when I approached him. "Good goin', boy." His voice was weak. "I knew you the one."

"But now it's gone."

"Not really. All these people who felt it, they got a piece of it. All these folks who love the Dodgers much as you or me, they all got a little bit of the Heart of Brooklyn living inside them. Their dreams are still alive."

"But—"

"See," Henry continued, "now there's the possibility that somehow, someday, it'll come back, come back whole again. It'll come back. It ain't dead, Eli. It's just changed. Maybe into a million seeds. You know what happens when you plant a million seeds?

"But now the Dodgers will leave Brooklyn." That's what Henry had told me the night before. I could hardly imagine how desolate the city would be without the Dodgers. It was unthinkable. Heartbreaking.

"Don't you worry, Eli. The magic's gonna sprout up into something new and different. I sure as heck won't be around to see it. Maybe not even you, Eli, young as you is. That Treasure is *old*! Some day, maybe it'll be soon, maybe long in the future, some little kids be playin' and they know as they roundin' third and headin' home, yeah they know that the Magic is still jumpin'." Henry smiled as he slipped back in his chair.

"Henry? Do you think I'll get my wish?"

He shook his head. "The Treasure never did give people their wishes," he said quietly. "That just an old wives' tale."

"Oh," I said, my heart sinking.

Henry looked me in the eye. "What it does give is your heart's desire. That's not necessarily the same thing." His head slumped to his chest.

"Henry!" I cried. I grabbed his arm. I called to Jackie and and Betty, "We gotta get a doctor!"

Henry rallied and looked up. "No. No doctor. I'm only weary that's all. Gotta get me some sleep. I got a date with the Sandman." He half sang and half spoke the beginning of a poem:

The Sandman walks abroad tonight,
With his canvas sack o' dreams filled tight
Over the roofs of the little town,
The golden face of the moon looks down.
Each Mary and Willy and Cora and Ned
Is sound asleep in some cozy bed,

When the Sandman opens his magic sack
To select the dreams from his wonder pack.

"That's Langston Hughes," Henry said. "Used to be a buddy of mine."

Henry gazed at me and Kenny and Jackie. He seemed happy and at peace. He took one last look around Ebbets Field and closed his eyes. He sighed once, and then breathed no more.

I burst out crying, my arms around the old man and my head resting by his heart.

Chapter 21

TWO DAYS LATER, YANKEE STADIUM was packed. The Dodgers had lost the sixth game, and now this final, seventh game would determine the champion. Jackie had gotten Kenny and me box seats near the Dodger dugout.

Jackie couldn't play cause of a pulled tendon, but it was a great game anyway. The greatest one ever. By the bottom of the sixth, the Dodgers were leading 2 to 0. The Yankees had Gil McDougald on first and Billie Martin on second. Then Yogi Berra came up to bat.

Kenny looked at me. I could tell he was thinking the same thing as me and all the Dodger fans. "Oh no. Here it comes. Not again."

Yogi took a few practice swings. Yogi always pulled the ball toward right field so the whole outfield shifted way over to the right. But Yogi swung late and hit the ball hard straight down the left field line.

Sandy Amoros was caught way out of position. It looked like two runs would score for sure. Amoros raced toward the left field line. Running at top speed, he stuck out his right, gloved hand. The ball landed in the glove!

Amoros took a few quick, little steps to avoid colliding with the fence, and then rocketed a perfect throw to Pee Wee Reese near third base.

Reese relayed the ball to Gil Hodges at first. The ball got there before Gil McDougald could get back to the bag. He was out. A double play!

Amaros had made one of the greatest catches in baseball history. The Dodger fans went absolutely berserk.

Kenny and I jumped up and down and screamed ourselves hoarse. At that moment, we knew the Dodgers were gonna win the Series. We just knew it.

In the bottom of the ninth inning, a woman approached our seats. She was wearing a white dress. She looked familiar.

"Eli?"

I nodded yes.

It was Aunt Esther! She said she saw the photos and stories about me in the papers and tracked me down. "I've dreamed about you hundreds of times over the last eleven years. I searched all over, but I could never find you."

I felt shy. I looked down at the ground.

She put her hands on my shoulder. "You can live with me and my husband. You know that, don't you?"

I nodded. Somehow, deep inside, I did know that. I pointed at Kenny. "Can Kenny come, too?"

She looked at Kenny, whose shining eyes were focused on the field. She turned back to me and smiled. "Aaron and I always dreamt of having two kids."

Just then, Elston Howard hit a grounder to Pee Wee

Reese at shortstop. Reese threw to Hodges. Howard was out and the game was over!

The deliriously happy Dodgers piled on pitcher Podres near the mound.

My aunt embraced me, tears flowing down her cheeks.

My insides were warm. It was like spring sunshine was spreading throughout my body. It was a sensation I didn't remember ever experiencing before. It felt like being home.

We stood there together quietly, our arms around each other, as the Dodger fans all around us went crazy with joy.

The Dodgers had beaten the Yankees at last. It was the happiest day in Brooklyn history. No more "wait till next year." This *was* next year!

Aunt Esther and I continued to hug as confetti fell all around us.

Epilogue

A UNT ESTHER REPORTED REIGER to the police, and told them all about the Hole and his beatings. Reiger went to jail for child abuse. The orphanage was shut down, and all the kids were adopted or placed in foster homes.

Kenny and I never did find the five hundred dollars Henry had hidden somewhere in the winding corridors below Ebbets Field.

A few years later, it was all over. The Brooklyn Dodgers were no more. Ebbets Field was no more. Just like Pigtown was no more. Just like the Treasure was no more. The Dodgers moved to Los Angeles in 1958, and Ebbets Field was torn down in 1960. It was destroyed by a wrecking ball grotesquely painted to look like a baseball.

Kenny and I went to the park that cold February day. We needed to witness the destruction first hand. I felt each smash of the wrecking ball echo in my own chest. I was glad Kenny was there with me. We had lived together with

Aunt Esther and Uncle Aaron ever since she had found me. It was comforting to have him standing next to me as the walls collapsed and the beams fell, and Ebbets Field was reduced to dust, burying Henry's money and a million memories.

In 2015, I made a pilgrimage back to the site of the park. I was now seventy-one years old, about the same age as Henry in 1955. I thought of how proud Henry and Jackie and Roy Campanella and those other pioneering black players would've been if they knew Barack Obama was president. In a way, they helped pave the way for him to be elected.

A cluster of drab, thirty-story tall apartment houses now rises where Ebbets Field once stood. A graffiti-covered sign identifies them as "EBBETS FIELD APARTMENTS." Another sign nearby reads, "NO BALL PLAYING ALLOWED."

I walked along the sidewalk at the foot of the buildings, imagining the way the ballpark used to exist right there. The most magical team that ever played baseball played at this very spot. Jackie Robinson stole home here. Henry Jenkins guarded this place for forty-three years. The Treasure he called "the Heart of Brooklyn" rested here for God knows how long before that.

I paused to watch a bunch of boys playing basketball across the street. Most of the kids around here these days are into basketball, not baseball. I continued walking and entered a concrete courtyard at the base of the apartment towers.

I took a baseball out of my pocket and looked at it. It was the one Jackie Robinson autographed for me on the day I saved him. I read Jackie's inscription out loud. "To Eli. Keep swinging. Your friend, Jackie Robinson." I smiled and put the ball back in my pocket, and walked and thought.

The Treasure's been gone for sixty years now. But, you know, the Magic is hard to kill. I watched a few children playing stickball in a narrow space between two of the apartment buildings. Yeah, I thought, the kids are still swinging. The old folks are still dreaming. Old Henry was right. The Heart of Brooklyn didn't die. It's not far away. You can hear it in the shouts of the children. You can sense it in the hearts of the people, in the songs, in the memories, in the land of possibility. It rests near third base, waiting to come home, waiting to come home.

I crossed the street and walked away from Ebbets Field Apartments. I sang to myself as I walked.

Did you see Jackie Robinson hit that ball?
Well he hit it, yeah, and that ain't all.
He's going home.
Yes, yes, Jackie's real gone.
Yes, yes, Jackie's real gone.

As I turned the corner, I saw a pigeon circling over me. The sunlight was in my eyes so I couldn't be sure, but I could swear he had a blue head. He flew toward the buildings. The bird swooped down and landed on top of the Ebbets Field Apartments sign.

I smiled and walked down the street, heading home.

The End

Acknowledgments

THANK YOU TO MY FATHER, HERBERT SEIDMAN, who took me to Ebbets Field to watch the Dodgers play in their final season in Brooklyn when I was four years old, and to my mother, Phoebe Seidman, who for many decades indulged our love of sports with generosity and good humor.

Thank you to my beloved wife, Rachael Resch, for her constant support.

Gratitude to Harley Patrick and Paloma Books for bringing this book to reality.

And thank you to the Heart of Brooklyn and all who help keep her alive.

About the Author

RICHARD SEIDMAN IS THE AUTHOR OF *World Cup Mouse, Mr. McFunny's Soccer Jokes for Kids* and *Mr. McFunny's Summer Olympics Jokes for Kids*, and several screenplays for family films. He also wrote one book for grown-ups, *A New Oracle of Kabbalah: Mystical Teachings of the Hebrew Letters*. He lives in Ashland, Oregon, USA with his wife and chickens and a baseball not signed by Jackie Robinson.

Visit Richard online at: *www.richardseidman.com.*

www.palomabooks.com

97914374R00071

Made in the USA
San Bernardino, CA
26 November 2018